Never Cross

D1538450

Trust Issues Book 3

Tamicka Higgins

© 2017

Disclaimer

All rights reserved. No part of this publication may be reproduced, distributed, or transmitted in any form or by any means, including photocopying, recording, or other electronic or mechanical methods, without the prior written permission of the publisher, except in the case of brief quotations embodied in critical reviews and certain other noncommercial uses permitted by copyright law.

This is a work of fiction. Names, places, characters and events are all fictitious for the reader's pleasure. Any similarities to real people, places, events, living or dead are all coincidental.

This book contains sexually explicit content that is intended for ADULTS ONLY (+18).

Chapter 1

Kayla just could not believe the words that she had just heard from her girl, Myesha. As she was heading home from dropping Marcus off at his mother's house, she had simply planned for her 20 to 30 minute ride by taking the street way, as being a little time where she could think to herself. Now, she wound up on the phone with Myesha, which was just fine. While basically updating her on what was going on with Marcus after sitting in the hospital for so many hours, she was now putting the peddle to the metal and trying to get home as quickly as possible.

"Girl, no," Kayla said. "I hope it ain't what I think it is."

"You mean, them?" Myesha asked. "I am so sorry, girl. Kayla, I ain't…I ain't…I ain't think when I was riding by your house that it might be them. Girl, what you want me to do? You know what? Let's just hang up and I can call the police or something."

Police? Oh hell no.

"No!" Kayla said, quickly responding to what Myesha was saying. "No, no. Myesha, girl, what is you thinking? You know that somebody gon' wind up dead if you call the damn police. And what if you call them and it ain't even what we think it is?"

There was no doubt in Kayla's mind at this point. There were just too many coincidences for her to think for one second that whatever car Myesha had seen outside of her house was the same car that Marcus had said he had seen when the bullets started to fly into his apartment – maybe even the same car that Latrell and Linell said they had seen when they came in from playing in the snow earlier in the afternoon. Kayla's heart must have been pumping a good sixty miles an hour at this point. Suddenly, what would normally be a quick 20 minute trip across the east side of the city seemed like a road trip through a never ending urban jungle. Every block seemed twice as far and twice as long in distance; every stoplight seemed to last twice as long. There were even a few stoplights, like at the intersection of 30ᵗʰ Street and Emerson Avenue, that Kayla slowly rolled across since there were no cars coming. At the front of her mind were Latrell and Linell. No matter what, she could not let anything happen to her little brother and sister.

Kayla began to feel guilty that she had ignored her family when they had been calling her earlier while she was with Marcus. It was getting to be so much to think about that she was practically breaking a sweat – practically imagining herself as being in one of those true crime specials that you turn on the television and watch at night. Kayla just could not let something like that happen. And, God willing, she would pull up in front of the house and find that it was all just a big overreaction. No matter how big the city or how small the town, a black car is nothing unusual or usual the least bit, in any way. Still, though, Kayla could feel in her heart – deep down in her soul – that she was not wrong. Her woman's intuition was kicking in. She only wished that it had kicked in much earlier, like when Marcus brought up the idea of moving to Atlanta, or when he was constantly checking out of his patio door.

Myesha rambled on in the background, but Kayla was not listening. Well, she tried to listen, but it was proving very hard to really focus on the words that were coming through to her ears. Eventually, she just had to stop it all.

"Myesha," Kayla said. "Girl, I'mma have to hit you up when I get there or something. I swear to God. I hope they ain't do nothing with my family. Not Latrell and Linell. Shit, shit, shit. Girl, let me call my mama phone and see if she answers."

"Okay, okay, girl," Myesha said. "You right. Call your mama. I hope everything turn out okay. Let me know, okay?"

Kayla did not even bother answering Myesha's question. Rather, she just pulled the phone down from the side of her face and hung up. Curse words practically slipped out of her mouth as she scrolled through her call log and looked for her last MISSED CALL from her mother. When she found it, she frantically pressed her name and called. Each ring was loud and twice as terrifying as the previous ring; the longer the ringing went on, the harder and more forceful Kayla's heart pumped.

"Answer, answer, answer," Kayla said, over and over again between rings.

Eventually, the line picked up.

"Mama?" Kayla said. "Hello? Hello?"

"Kayla?" her mother Rolanda said. It was obvious to Kayla that her mother's voice was trembling. In fact, she had never heard her mother sound so timid. Any other time she answered the phone, there was without a doubt a little tension and maybe even bitterness in her voice. Noticing the difference, Kayla knew why there was a change. At this very moment, as she drove as quickly as she could down 30th Street, across the east side of the city and heading toward the west side, she knew that her worst fears were coming to be a reality. At that very moment, she wished that she had warned her mother before she left the house about what Latrell and Linell had said they had seen while they were playing out in the snow. How could she not tell her mother, if nothing else? The guilt that had consumed Kayla was starting to feel like walls on either side of her body slowly inching toward one another. The night sky seemed so dark and the city seemed so dead, Kayla rarely passing by headlights in the oncoming lane. Never had her drive seemed so terrifying and eerie.

"Yeah, Mama, yeah," Kayla said. "It's me."

"Kayla, baby," Rolanda said, her voice still sounding timid. "You still at the hospital?"

"What's wrong, Mama?" Kayla asked. "I am on my way home right now. I swear, I am on my way home."

"Fuckin' ask her," a man said, in the background. "You fuckin' hear me, bitch? Ask that bitch what fuckin' room that nigga stayin' in and stop with all the lovey dovey bullshit. Ask her."

Kayla almost stopped breathing for a moment as she heard the man in the background make that command.

"Mama!" Kayla yelled into the phone. "Who is that? Who is there with you?"

"Kayla, these niggas…" Rolanda began saying. Her voice trailed off, making Kayla worry even more. Within seconds, all she could hear was her mother crying (something she rarely had seen let alone heard) and curse words spewing out of a man's mouth.

Suddenly, a man picked up her mother's cell phone and began to talk into it.

"Call the fuckin' police if you want to," he said. "And when they get here, they gon' find three dead bodies."

"No," Kayla said. "Please don't. No, no, no."

"Tell us where the fuck that nigga at and you won't have to worry about all that," the man demanded.

Tears now strolled down both of Kayla's cheeks. She had always seen situations like this play out on television. She had even read them in words on pages in books she would get from the library. However, not for one second did Kayla ever, in a million years, think that she would be one of the main characters when something like this went down. This kind of stuff just did not happen to her.

Kayla blew straight through a stoplight, not even noticing that the light had been red until she was a good block or two passed it.

"Please, don't hurt them," Kayla pleaded.

Just as Kayla was starting to bring up Marcus, she knew that if she at least waited until she got there to say whatever she was going to say, then maybe she would be able to keep whatever nigga this was from killing her mother, brother, and sister. If only, Kayla thought. However, she still had several miles to go before she would even get to her side of the city. On top of that, her situation was even worse in a lot of ways because with where she was now, there was no highway for her to get onto that would make her trip that much quicker. In so many ways, Kayla felt helpless, so she knew that she had to play what few cards she had been dealt in this entire situation to her advantage.

"Just tell us where the fuck the nigga is," the dude said. "Tell us that and won't nobody here get hurt, simple as that. Now…tell me where the fuck that nigga Marcus is. What hotel room?"

Us? As in more than one of you? Upon hearing that particular word choice and understanding right away what he was really saying, Kayla almost felt as if she could have had a stroke or heart attack.

"I am coming," Kayla said. "Just don't hurt them. I am about to be there, I am about to be there. Just don't hurt them."

"Whatever," the man said.

Whatever?

Just then, Kayla could hear a gunshot go off through the phone. It was so loud that the speaker on her phone vibrated in her ear, painfully. Kayla screamed as she could hear the muffled yells of terror of her mother, brother, and sister. She was now sobbing uncontrollably.

"You hear that," the dude came back on the phone saying. "Next bullet ain't gon' go into the damn ceiling. Show up with some police and find out."

"I am coming, I am coming," Kayla said. "Just please, don't kill them."

Rather than responding to Kayla, the man simply hung up the phone. Kayla, without even thinking, threw her phone down onto the passenger side seat. While still gripping the wheel with one hand, she would alternate arms and wipe the tears away from her face.

"God, oh God," Kayla said to herself. "If anything happen to Mama or Latrell and Linell, oh God. Please, please, please."

Kayla continued driving as fast as she could west on 30th Street. If an intersection with a stoplight was clear, she did not give a second thought to going on across. So much of the city was eerie and dead on this cold winter night. As Kayla came closer to Meridian Street – the street that divides the city between its east and west sides – tiny little white snowflakes began to land on her windshield. To make this worse, Kayla could hear the wind blowing and colliding with the sides of the car. Instantly, having lived in a snowy place like this all of her life, she eased off of the accelerator just to be careful. The last thing she needed was to slide while she was driving.

Once Kayla crossed Meridian Street, she knew that she only had about a mile and a half more to go before pulling up outside of the house. She just hoped to God that she would not be a mile and a half too late.

***

Myesha felt restless to say the least when she dropped her phone onto her bed. She had been chilling in her room after returning from doing the book exchange with her classmate. Even though Kayla was not technically her family or blood relative in any way, Myesha had always been closer to Kayla than she was with a lot of people in her own family. If anything happened to Kayla or her family, she too would feel her pain. When Kayla cried, she cried.

"Oh my God, oh my God," Myesha said to herself over and over again. Before she knew it, she had dropped down to her knees on the side of her bed and was saying a little prayer. She only hoped that God was listening and that nobody would have to lose their life tonight. When she got up off of her knees, she paced back and forth in front of her bed. Of course, she wanted to do the right thing, which was to call the police. However, just like Kayla, Myesha knew that if she called the police, things would only escalate. Whoever was after Marcus clearly would either not be scared of the police or would make a really drastic move if their back was pushed against the wall.

Myesha just could not take her inaction anymore. Just like Kayla, she was starting to feel guilty. She remembered that when she had seen the car parked out front of Kayla's house, she had just assumed that it belonged to a man who Kayla's mother had over. Myesha felt so guilty right then for not mentioning sooner to Kayla that a car that she had never seen before was parked outside of her house. For this very reason, she knew that she had to do something.

Quickly, Myesha slid back into her boots then grabbed her coat and headed downstairs. As soon as she got to the bottom of the stairs, her mother caught her attention. Sitting in the living room on the couch across from the television, Myesha's mother, Brenda, had a crazy look written all over her face.

"Girl, where you running out to?" Brenda asked. "It's late and you know we probably going to be getting some more snow again tonight. Or, at least, that's what the news said. Maybe it is already flurrying, I don't know."

"I'll be right back, Mama," Myesha said to her mother, not wanting to take the time to explain.

Myesha headed out of the front door, not even entertaining the idea of holding a brief conversation with her mother. In fact, the only reason she had even responded to what her mother had said was out of respect. Rather, Myesha pushed through the cold Indiana wind. Little snow flurries fell from the sky and quickly got caught in her eye lashes. She shivered uncontrollably, feeling how much the temperature had dropped since she had been outside just a couple of hours earlier. The side of her face stung from the bitter, sharp wind; the sound of the inner city was a light, distant hum. Even to Myesha, this night seemed so quiet and cold and eerie.

Myesha climbed into her car and did not even bother with letting it warm up – she simply did not have the time to be doing all of that. Rather, as soon as she slammed her car door closed, she carefully pulled her car out of her parking spot and slowly drove down toward Kayla's house. This short distance, of mainly a block and a half or so, seemed oh so far. However, Myesha knew that she had to do something. Even if she could not call the police, she felt some sort of responsibility in case something did go down. Without even thinking of herself, she carefully drove down the snow-packed side street. She kept her eyes open for Kayla's house, on her left. It was crazy how something that would normally seem so close seemed so far away in times where somebody's life – that somebody being somebody close to you and who you know – was in the balance. Myesha shook her head side to side as words spilled out of her mouth – as she hoped that whoever was after Marcus would not do any harm to Kayla's family.

***

Kayla played it cool the last mile or so home. When she turned off of 30th Street and began to zigzag through the crunchy side streets of her neighborhood, she could not help but to be nervous. Just like Myesha, her head shook from the guilt. However, while her head was shaking, her mind could not help but to play over and over again to itself the man's voice that she had heard just minutes ago on the phone. The tears had started to slow down on her face, but they were still steady enough to where she needed to wipe them away from her face as she sniffled and begged God for nothing to happen to her mother, brother, and sister.

Kayla passed Myesha's house and noticed that Myesha's car was not out front. However, she could not preoccupy herself with why that would be at that very moment. If it had been any other time, she would have picked the phone up and called her girl to see what she was up to. Kayla's focus – only focus – was getting down these slick side streets without sliding into a car or up onto a sidewalk.

As Kayla rolled through the last intersection before crossing into her block, her heart pounded. Never had her hood seemed so scary. Everything sat so still; few lights were on in any of her neighbors' houses. Kayla could not help but to press the accelerator just a little bit when she was coming up on her house. Her eyes could not pull themselves away from the two-story structure.

"I am here, y'all," Kayla said, looking at her house. "I am here."

Kayla could see that only the living room light was on. There was also some sort of movement going on, as she could see with the silhouettes moving behind the curtains. After taking a quick glance around and seeing that there were no cops there, she prayed that such a fact would have been the saving grace, so to speak, for her mother, brother, and sister. She quickly turned her car off and climbed out.

As soon as Kayla stepped up onto the sidewalk, she heard the ever so light tap of a car horn – light in the way it was tapped but still loud on a quiet winter night like this. Her head snapped out of her daze and looked to her right. A car not too far away was flashing its lights. She paused, right there on the sidewalk as it passed her house, and squinted, trying to see who could be in this car and wondering if maybe the guy that had been on the phone with her mother was now in a car instead. However, soon enough, she noticed a black car, parked ever so casually as if it belonged in the neighborhood. It was parked a couple of spots down from Kayla, looking menacing and much like what Marcus had described when she found his shot body on his bedroom floor earlier in the day.

The car further up the block flashed its light again. Just then, a woman got out and was waving her arms. Kayla could see it was her best friend Myesha. Soon enough, Myesha was rushing around the front of her own car then up onto the sidewalk.

"Girl, what the fuck are you doing here?" Kayla asked.

"Kayla, I am so sorry," Myesha said, apologetically. "I can't believe I saw that car earlier and didn't even think to call you and tell you, and this was after you told me about Marcus' place being shot up like that. How could I not do that?"

"They in there right now, girl," Kayla said.

Myesha's head snapped toward the house, her eyes looking in terror.

"Right now?" she asked. "Are you serious?"

"Girl, I am so scared I don't know what to do," Kayla said. "Yes, after I hung up with you, I called my mama and she answered. She clearly sounded scared as shit. Next thing I know, some dude is taking the phone from her and telling me that he want to know what room Marcus is in. He said that if I call the police, they would show up and find three dead bodies."

Myesha's hand immediately covered her mouth as she shook her head back and forth. "Girl, I am so sorry," she said. "I am so, so, so, so sorry."

Kayla looked back at the house. "Girl, I gotta go in there now," she said.

"Girl, what you gon' do, though?" Myesha asked.

Kayla shook her head. "I don't know," she said. "But I can't stand out here talking and I can't call the police or nothing. I gotta go in there."

"What if they take you hostage or something?" Myesha asked. "Girl, I don't know now. I don't know about this, Kayla. Them niggas might be crazy or something."

"I know," Kayla said, bravely.

"But what you gon' tell them?" Myesha asked. "You said that you took Marcus home. You gon send them over to his mama house? You know niggas would kill him and his mama."

Kayla did not want to think about something so terrible happening. Her only focus at that very moment was stopping whoever was up in her house with her mother, brother, and sister from pulling the trigger again – pulling a trigger and putting a bullet into someone's head. A tear rolled down her cheek, almost freezing as it became smaller and smaller toward where her chin rounded under to her neck.

"I know, I know," Kayla said, starting to walk up the walkway. "But I gotta do something. Latrell and Linell. Girl, don't be out here for them to see you. Don't."

"I…," Myesha said, her words trailing off. She had not known what she had run out of the house to come down to Kayla's house to do, but she knew that she had to do something. Seeing that Kayla was already gone, headed up toward the front porch, Myesha quickly backed away and hurried back down the sidewalk and to her own car.

To Kayla, her house seemed so big and cold and mysterious. She did not know if she would open the front door and find one man with a gun, or two or three men. Whatever she found, though, she knew it would not be good. The voice on the phone – whoever it belonged so – sounded as if it were laced with pure evil.

Kayla wanted to rush right into the house, getting her keys out. However, she hesitated. The last thing she wanted to do was anything that would make whoever was inside pull the trigger. Hesitantly, Kayla pressed her house key into the front door. At least a dozen prayers that she had heard throughout her life raced through her head while she fidgeted with the key and lock in the cold, as the wind was not making this entire ordeal any better because of how cold it was.

As soon as Kayla pushed her front door open and the light of the living room touched her feet, her eyes met with a tall, brown-skin dude. He looked at her so coldly, almost not blinking. Kayla, remembering that for the safety of her family, knew that she needed to make sure that she did not overact the least bit.

"Hurry up and get the fuck in here," the man standing over her mother said.

Kayla nodded. "Okay," she said, softly.

Kayla stepped into the living room and softly pushed the door closed, taking a deep breath as she did. When she turned around, her eyes could not help but to land on Latrell and Linell. There they were, huddled in a corner, with another dude standing over them. He grinned – a sarcastic grin, really – while he gripped his gun. Kayla shook, now seeing that there were two niggas in her house and they both had guns. Her heart was beating so fast that her body was practically shaking as the door shut.

"Lock the fuckin' door, bitch," the man standing over Rolanda said. "Don't act like you fuckin' brand new or nothin'."

Kayla did as she was told, locking the front door then turning around. Now, with her eyes better adjusted to the light, she could see the faces of the two dudes. The one standing over Rolanda was noticeably taller than the dude who was standing over Latrell and Linell. If Kayla did not know any better, she would have thought that he was mixed with some sort of Hispanic. There were tattoos on his neck, looking as if they were crawling out of the top of his shirt. When he half-assed smiled at Kayla, she could feel his eyes looking at her shapely body – looks that made her feel so vulnerable.

The other guy, who was standing over Latrell and Linell, was more-so the bulkier of the two. Dressed in black as well, the muscles of his upper body bulged in his shirt; the veins in his hands were so pronounced that they could not be missed. He was also much darker in skin complexion, looking only a shade or two, if that, lighter than Marcus. Either way, the two men were equally scary at the same time.

"Please, don't hurt my kids," Rolanda pleaded. "I am beggin' you, please."

"Shut the fuck up bitch wit' all that fuckin' winning you been doin'," the guy standing over Kayla's mother said. "Before I give you something to really cry about."

Just then, he smiled and pointed his gun across the room. The direct line of the barrel was at Latrell and Linell. A scream slipped out of both Rolanda and Kayla's mouth at the same moment.

"Now," the man said. "Tell me what fuckin' room that nigga in before y'all bodies lyin' out on this nice carpet and shit. Hate for somebody to have to get killed up in this real nice house, wouldn't it?"

He nodded at his partner. He nodded back and looked down at Latrell and Linell. The looks of terror and fear and uncertainty were written all over their faces. It was clearly hurting Rolanda to the very core to even think about how helpless she was about the situation. Thoughts still bounced around in her mind about lunging across the room. However, with two dudes who both had guns. There was just no possible way doing such a thing would work out in anyone's favor.

Kayla froze up instantly, wishing that she had prepared some sort of answer to that question before coming through the door. Upon processing what had just been said to her, she remembered hearing it on the phone. She hated – a feeling that tore away at the pits of her stomach – that she had not taken the time to think up something to say while she was riding over from dropping Marcus off at Ms. Lorna's house. No matter what, she just could not think straight no matter how hard she tried to do so.

"Bitch, I know you fuckin' hear me talkin' to your dumb ass," the man standing over her mother said. "What fuckin' room is that nigga Marcus in so we can go see his ass?"

"Yeah," the dude standing over Latrell and Linell said. "We just wanna give him a little get well card is all." He chuckled and looked at his partner, who then chuckled too.

Just then, Rolanda felt the still-cold tip of the barrel of the gun press into the temple of her head. She whimpered Jesus' name over and over again, tears practically streaming down the side of her face.

"Kayla!" Rolanda yelled. "What the fuck you don' got us caught up in? Huh? Who are these niggas?"

Kayla tried to find the words to speak, but she just could not pull them to the front of her mind. She did not even have the answers to those questions. And even if she did, she knew better than to say anything that would sound even remotely bad or antagonizing about the two dudes in the room with the power – the two niggas with the guns and a clear itch to blow somebody's fucking brains out.

"Tell them, Kayla!" Rolanda demanded. "These niggas is crazy, I swear. They just don't give a fuck. I told them that we don't know and they was just so convinced that we did. I don't even know why they doin' this shit. Good God, Kayla, just tell them what fuckin' room that little nigga is in so these crazy motherfuckers can get what they want and get the fuck up out of my house. Tell them, goddammit!"

Kayla looked back and forth at both sides of the living room. She was well aware that she knew Marcus was at his mother's house. However, at the same time, she knew that there was no way she could tell either of these crazy niggas where Miss Lorna lived. It was becoming very obvious, very fast that whatever shit her boyfriend Marcus had gotten himself caught up in ran deeper than the typical hustlers standing around on the corner.

With her eyes darting back and forth, Kayla blurted out the number to the hospital room where Marcus had been. "Eight o three," she said.

"Get your sexy lil' ass over here," the man standing over Rolanda said.

Just then, before Kayla could even move herself, the man stepped across the room and grabbed her. In one quick swoop, Kayla could feel the strength of the man's grip. He quickly pulled her away from the front doorway and down to the floor. Next thing Kayla knew, she was almost lying on her back and now looking up, in both directions, into the eyes of both niggas, as she was smack dab in the middle of the room.

"Eight o three, huh?" the one standing over Rolanda said. "Ay, nigga, you hear that?"

"Yep," the guy standing over Latrell and Linell said. "Up on the eighth floor."

"Look here," the other one said. He then pushed Rolanda to the side, her head slamming into a large vase that was against the other wall. She quickly started to get back up so she could be aware. Her focus, as any mother's would be, was the welfare of her three children. "You betta not be fuckin' with us you little bitch. You hear me, Kayla. You betta not be fuckin' wit us. If we go to this fuckin' hospital room and this nigga ain't there, we gon head right back on over here and put y'all niggas in the fuckin' hospital. Try me."

Kayla, who was nervous that she had just told a bold face lie, nodded her head. "Okay, okay," she said. "I told you what room he in. I told you. He at Methodist in room eight o three."

The two men looked at one another then shook their heads.

"If this nigga ain't in this hospital room, we gon' be right back over here to have a little meeting with the family again," the guy standing over Rolanda said. "Swear to God."

Just then, before any of them knew it, the guy standing over Rolanda hit Rolanda in the head with the butt of his gun. As curse words slipped out of her mouth, Rolanda could not help but to feel a little woozy from the blow she had just taken. It was one thing to have the end of the barrel pressed into her temple. However, it was another thing to be completely bludgeoned in the head as if she was some rag doll or some crack head out in the streets.

After a deep wince slipped out of Rolanda's mouth, her reflexes kicked in. Without even thinking, the mother started swinging at the legs of the gunman. Her blows, which were weak on account of the fact that she was slowly getting dizzy, hit in some places on his thighs. Others missed altogether as tears flooded her eyes and made it that much harder for her to really see what she was doing. All Rolanda knew was that her rage had built up. These two niggas had come into her house with guns and basically had held her family captive for something they did not even have anything to do with. It all just made no sense, especially since Rolanda had only found out about Marcus having any sort of problems at all when Kayla came home in the afternoon from the hospital saying that his place had been shot up and that he had been hit in the shoulder.

The man standing over Rolanda laughed at the older – at least older compared to him – woman's attempts to push him back away from her after he pistol whipped her. She had a little strength to her and he would give her that. However, she just did not have what it took to really push him away like that. Rather, the dude chuckled and just started kicking at Rolanda's swinging fists. With the tips of his shoes colliding with her fists, Rolanda could not help but to feel the pain. It was just to much.

Kayla felt another tear drop roll down her cheek. Even with all of the differences that she and her mother had always had, especially lately, the last thing she wanted to do was to see her get pistol whipped in front of her own children. No child deserved to see such a thing go down. Just then, as Kayla looked into the eyes of the man standing above her mother then into the eyes of the man standing above Latrell and Linell, she knew what it was really like to look into the eyes of evil. And, to say the least, these eyes of evil were part of an overall ugly face.

"This bitch really think she doin' something, huh?" he said, looking down at Rolanda. Rolanda could not help but to begin slowing down with how fast and how hard she was trying to hit him. She could feel her head throbbing out of control while he just kicked her like it was all fun and games.

"What the fuck is wrong with you?" Kayla asked, loudly and assertively. "I told you the fuckin' hospital room number. I told you! Why the fuck are you still here? Why the fuck are you still doin' this shit to us? I told you the fuckin' hospital room number – eight o three."

The man stopped kicking at the very same time that Rolanda stopped trying to hit him. Instead, Rolanda began to sob as the pain in her head was getting to be so great that she just might fall unconscious right there on the floor. She wept and wept, every so often making eye contact with Latrell and Linell. To say the very least, this was a woman who felt humiliated and embarrassed in front of her own children.

"Oh, she think she bad, huh?" the man standing over Rolanda said, looking at Kayla. "She think she tough and shit over there talkin' shit to me. Look here, bitch, we'll leave when we fuckin' feel like leaving."

"Stop!" Linell yelled, breaking her timid, little girl silence. "You're hurting my mama! You're hurting my mama!"

The man blocking Latrell and Linell into the corner by the couch looked at his partner.

"Nigga," he said. "What the fuck is you doin', bruh? We need to get the fuck outta here before one of these fuckin' neighbors hears this shit or something. Let's get down to this fuckin' hospital so we can get that nigga Marcus. Stop fuckin' round, nigga."

The man standing over Rolanda nodded, realizing that his partner was right.

"Aight, aight," he said, still nodding. "We gon' go ahead and get the fuck up out here."

He stepped toward the front door, leading Rolanda and Kayla to think that he was truly headed out of the front door and that his partner would soon follow. However, for Kayla at least, things would soon change. Before Kayla could even realize what was going on, the man who had been standing over her mother had grabbed her up off of the floor. She now stood up, looking almost into his cold, uncaring eyes. He smiled.

"Little sexy mama," he said then leaned in.

Kayla shivered – cringed, really – at feeling his hot breath on her ear as he talked so low that it was almost as if he were whispering.

"Let this nigga not be in this hospital room when we get down there," he said then chuckled. "And you know what? You know what?"

"What?" Kayla asked, angrily. There was nothing she wanted more in the world at that very moment than to be free from his grip – to be free from the risk of having a bullet in her head.

He chuckled. "If this nigga ain't in this fuckin' hospital room," he continued. "I'mma really give you somethin' to cry about. When you sleepin' at night, or maybe just walking down the street, you gon' see me again. I never forget a face, especially not a pretty one. Better yet, I never forget a body…especially a body like this one." At the end of his sentence, he slapped Kayla's ass so hard that her ass cheek stung. A little gasp slipped out of her lips, but she would not let him see her bow down too much. She knew that she could be stronger than that, even if she did not believe it herself completely at that very moment. "I'mma come get in that pussy," the man added. "I'mma come get deep in that pussy and really do some shit to you that I know your boyfriend ain't done."

Just as Kayla wanted to push him away from her and yell "fuck you," she could feel his warm, wet tongue slither out of his mouth. He ran the tip along the curves of her ear then into the inside. What usually might be a "spot" for Kayla had just become one of the most disgusting and vile things ever.

The man then gripped Kayla's chin and turned her face toward his. "Look at me," he whispered. Kayla did as she was told – looked at him but did not keep eye contact for too long a period of time. "I can promise you that," he added.

Rolanda looked at this tall thug practically sexually violate her daughter. She hated how helpless she felt, feeling the bump practically popping out of her own head from where she had been pistol whipped. She wanted to lunge forward so bad that the temptation was almost killing her.

The man pushed Kayla back down to the floor just before pulling the front door open and stepping out into the winter. "Come on nigga," he said to his partner.

The other guy – the one who had been standing over Latrell and Linell – snickered as he pointed the gun at the four of them and backed out of the living room. As soon as the two men were out of the door, darting across the snow covered from yard to their car, Kayla quickly jumped up and pushed the door shut. Moving frantically, she locked it. Kayla turned around and looked at her mother, brother, and sister. That feeling of guilt – the one where the concrete walls were slowly inching toward her helpless body in a figurative room where there was no escape – consumed the very core of her. Quickly, she helped her mother up off of the floor.

Rolanda, who was so deep in her feelings that she really could not think all that straight, got onto her feet as quickly as she could. Without even thinking, she pushed Kayla away and went straight for Latrell and Linell. She hugged them tightly then turned and looked at her adult daughter.

"Kayla!" she yelled. "What the fuck is goin' on? What the fuck is that nigga Marcus caught up in that these niggas would be busting in my fuckin' door and doin' my family like this? I told him that we ain't know what hospital room he was in. Girl, what the fuck have you done?"

Just then, because of where Kayla was now standing in comparison to her mother, she could see where she had been pistol whipped on the side of her head. Blood slowly gushed out as the bump from the impact practically grew right before her eyes. She sniffled while a couple of tears ran down her cheek.

"Mama, I am sorry," Kayla said. "I am so sorry."

"Girl, this just don't make no damn sense," Rolanda said. "We practically up in here getting' our asses beat and shit while we bein' held hostage and your ass is so far up that nigga's ass that you can't even answer the damn phone."

Kayla started to speak, but her mother cut her off.

"Kayla, I called you like ten, twenty fuckin' times over the last couple hours," Rolanda said. "I know that you had to see us callin' at least a couple of them times. Damn, girl. You so on that nigga's nuts that you don't even give a fuck about your fuckin' family. You sittin' up in the hospital room with him and couldn't step out for one fuckin' second to answer at least one of our calls?"

Kayla looked down at Latrell and Linell. She had never seen the two of them look so terrified in their life. Without even thinking, she quickly stepped forward to hug them – first Linell. Her hug was broken, however, by her both. Rolanda, still very much in the heat of the moment with what had happened, pushed Kayla back.

"Girl, you don't love us," Rolanda said. "Fuckin' look at us. And you wasn't even here for most of it, couldn't even answer the phone. Then you wanna come home acting like you was here with them fuckin' crazy ass niggas for three hours and shit."

Kayla was even reaching her breaking point, not only with herself but with how her mother was acting like everything that had happened tonight was her doing. She wiped the stray tears away from her face as she found the strength to say what she needed to say.

"Mama, you ain't gotta say all that," Kayla said. "I didn't know that y'all was calling to tell me that there were two men here. I ain't know."

"Girl, whatever," Rolanda said. She then walked Latrell and Linell into the dining room and told them to sit back down while she went into the kitchen. Just then, Kayla looked up. From what she could see, it seemed that her mother was just getting dinner ready when the two guys showed up. There were plates on the dining room table – three plates to be exact – and cups with a jug of what looked like Kool-Aid setting in the middle. Kayla tried to play over what could have happened in her mind, but was just coming up with too many blanks. She stepped into the dining room.

"How did they even get in?" Kayla asked.

Rolanda came walking back into the dining room. There was so much anger in her face that she looked as if she could have blown the roof of the house off if she wanted to.

"What the fuck you mean how did they get in?" Rolanda asked. "One came to the door, Kayla. And I thought it was some nigga I knew, so I went to open it. While he was pushing his way in here, the one that was holding my baby's over in the corner like they that damn Boko Haram over in Nigeria or something, the other one was pushing in the damn back door. The fuckin' back door is off the fuckin' hinges and shit."

"Mama, your head," Latrell said, pointing at his mother's wound.

"Don't worry about my head," Rolanda said. "I am just glad them niggas ain't do shit to you. That's all Mama is worried about, so don't you worry."

"Mama," Linell said. "Blood is running down the side of your face."

Rolanda, not even realizing that she was bleeding like that, raised her hand and dipped the tips of her fingers into her head. When she saw the rich red color that was her blood, her head just started shaking.

"Kayla!" she yelled. "This shit don't even make no damn sense. What the fuck has that nigga done got himself mixed up in? What the fuck is this shit? I mean…this shit don't even make no damn sense, I swear it don't."

Kayla did not know what she could say that would make the situation any better. Rather than speak, she rushed passed her mother and into the kitchen. She quickly got some ice cubes out of the freezer and wrapped them in a dish towel that she grabbed from a pile of recently washed towels that were setting on top of the dryer just inside the back porch. While she grabbed the towel, she looked at the back door and knew that no matter what, there was no way that they would be safe tonight in that house.

Kayla hurried back into the dining room and handed the towel with ice to her mother. Rolanda pressed it into the side of her forehead.

"Did you see that backdoor, Kayla?" she asked. "Did you see that shit? You already know that the landlord gon' get in our shit about that shit. You already know that white man already don't really like us like that with his racist ass. Once he see what the fuck happened to his property, he gon' get us up out of her for sure."

Kayla knew that she had to bring up the lie she had just told. In fact, the sooner she brought it up, the better she and her family would be. It would only be a matter of time – a short time – before the two niggas who had just left minutes ago would go to that hospital and find that Marcus was nowhere to be found. They then would be headed right back over to Kayla, to do exactly what they had said that they would do. Kayla could remember to well the look in both of their eyes. And she knew that they were serious about what they had said.

"Where was you, Kayla, huh?" Rolanda asked, sitting down at a chair. "Huh? Where was you?"

"I was taking Marcus home, Mama," Kayla answered. "The doctors went ahead and decided to let him go tonight, something about the hospital being crowded and them needing the space for people with real emergencies or something."

Rolanda quickly picked up on what she had just been told and what it would really mean.

"You took his ass home?" she asked, wanting clarification. "You just told them niggas that he was still in the hospital Kayla. They specifically said that if they get to the hospital and find that he ain't there, they gon' come back."

Hesitantly, Kayla nodded. "I know, I know," she said, nodding. "I didn't know what else to say to them. I wasn't going to give them Marcus' mama address so they could go over there and kill them."

"Why the fuck not?" Rolanda demanded to know. "They got our fuckin' address and we ain't even got shit to do with whatever the fuck Marcus did. How fucked up is that, Kayla? You try'na protect him and his family and shit while we over here getting our asses beat with pistols and shit. My nine-year-old kids just had the most horrific experience of their life and now you just done made it worse."

Kayla bit her bottom lip, trying her hardest to hold back tears.

"And now this bitch wanna break down and cry," Rolanda said, shaking her head. "Lord have mercy, you have got to be kidding me. I don't know what the fuck you cryin' for. You were here for only what? Twenty minutes of all this? We was stuck up in this fuckin' house for two fuckin' hours while we was callin' your ass and goin' straight to voicemail like we nothing. Marcus is okay, though. Thank you, Jesus. The world will be perfectly already as long as Kayla's Marcus is okay. Yeah, that's what matter. Oh God, girl, I don't know what the fuck you done got us involved in. I swear to God I don't."

Kayla knew that no matter how much she wanted to plead her case to her mother and explain that even she did not know all of this was going to happen, her heart would not stop thumping as long as she and her family were in that house. Methodist hospital was only a few minutes away driving on a clear day. Thanks to the snow, they had a little more time because people tended to drive a little slower.

"We gotta get outta this house," Kayla said. "They gon' go right down to that hospital and find that Marcus ain't there." Just then, Kayla had a quick flashback of the man who had been standing over her mother whispering in her ear and slapping her ass. "Mama, we gotta get Latrell and Linell out of this house before they come back. We gotta get outta here."

"Where we gon' go, Kayla?" Rolanda asked. "Huh? You act like I am rich or somethin' and we can just go move into a hotel or some shit. Where the fuck we gon' go in a hurry like this?"

Kayla did not have an answer to that question. All she could think about at that moment was how they needed to get the hell out of there before those dudes came back over. Quickly, she turned around and started to gather up Latrell and Linell's coats from the living room. Just as she grabbed Linell's coat off of the couch, there was a knock at the front door. Immediately, everybody's eyes cut to the front door; not a single word was said. Kayla felt her heart once again practically jump out of her chest. The last thing they felt like having at that moment was any visitors. They needed to get the hell out of that house as soon as possible.

Chapter 2

With Marcus being mad from how Kayla just put all the blame on him, his own mood was not in all that good of a state. To only make matters worse, with this being the first time he had ever had to wear a sling of any kind, he was just all sorts of uncomfortable. After watching Kayla pull off from the family room window of his mother's house, Marcus plopped down onto the couch. Right then, more than anything, he wanted to just go to sleep. Whatever the hospital had given him before surgery was starting to wear off and he was starting to feel a little sore. He had already decided that when he got up to Fort Wayne tomorrow, he would get over to the closest pharmacy to get his prescription filled for whatever pain relievers the doctor had prescribed to him.

Lorna came walking into the room. Like any mother, she was clearly very stressed over how much her life had changed in the last so many hours.

"Marcus!" Lorna barked, noticing how he was nodding off.

Marcus, hearing his mother's voice, lifted his head up. "What? What?" he said.

"I want the truth, Marcus," Lorna said. "I want the fuckin' truth. I know that you weren't going to tell me at the hospital, so that's why I really didn't push the topic like I wanted to when we were there. I don't care how bad it is. Just tell me so I can know just how bad it is exactly. What the hell is going on and why would anyone be after you and coming to shoot up your apartment like this? Tell me."

Marcus shook his head and groaned. The last person in the world that he ever wanted to talk to about that life was his mother. Sure, she had dated a couple of drug dealers off and on back when she was younger. However, as she matured and focused on being a mother and trying to have some stability, all of that became a distant memory. All of that became something that she heard her girlfriends bitching and moaning about. She thanked God every day that she did not make the wrong choices when she was young and get caught up in that lifestyle the way so many black women do.

"Marcus?" Lorna barked again. "I swear… I won't go off. I won't. I just wanna know how serious this shit is."

Marcus looked into his mother's eyes, appreciating how she was coming to him like he was a man rather than like he was a boy. While he did not really want to tell her, he figured he might as well go ahead and do so. In his mind, Hakim's boys were probably only trying to scare him. Rather, that is what he wanted to believe.

After Marcus told his mother Lorna the entire story – the part about the trip and the part about Hakim's girl, Tweety – he could not help but to see the dumbfounded look on her face. Lorna took a deep breath, now sitting on the couch across from her son, and slowly stood up by pressing the palms of her hands into her knees. She turned away, starting to walk back into the kitchen, but not before looking back at her son.

"Marcus," she said, shaking her head. "I love you and I really want you to know that. But, you know, I really did not raise you to be this way. Not to say I never thought you would have any problems. After all, as you should remember me telling you when you were growing up that life is very fragile and you cannot take anything for granted. But I really did want better for you. I wanted you to be better than your daddy and I damn sure didn't want you to get mixed up with your Uncle Roy and all that bullshit that nigga keeps going."

"Mama," Marcus said, calmly. "This ain't got nothin' to do with Uncle Roy, Mama. That's what makes this even worse, if it can get any worse. Uncle Roy always told me to stick close to your family and I really fu…" He caught himself, knowing that no matter how grown he got, his mother would in no way, shape, or form tolerate her son using language like that in her house, and especially not to her face. "Messed up," he finished. "This Hakim dude is actually somebody that I met through somebody that me, Brandon, and Juan know."

"Brandon and Juan," Lorna said, shaking her head and walking back into the kitchen. "How in the hell did I know them two niggas would have something to do with this shit?"

"Mama, it wasn't them," Marcus said. "You was at the hospital earlier when Kayla said that the two dudes came by her place asking for me. Brandon and Juan was there the entire time. Mama, I really don't think that it was them who did this. Plus, I know my boys and they wouldn't do no stuff like this."

As much as it pained Lorna to do this, she knew that if she was the rational parent that she always thought of herself as, she needed to think rationally even when it came to Brandon and Juan. She poured herself a glass of water and came back into the living room. She leaned against the doorway, her eyes looking her little boy up and down as she realized how much a few inches could have made in taking his life.

"Marcus," Lorna said, in a very stern tone. "I know you think you know everything at your age, cause I remember being there. The only difference is that I had a baby to take care of when I was your age. You didn't and that's what makes your ability to do something with your life a lot different. Okay, I will give you that maybe Brandon and Juan are not the actual guys who shot up your apartment. Okay, I can see that and as much as I don't trust them sneaky little fucks, I will admit that maybe they didn't pull the trigger. But you said this Hakim person is somebody that y'all met through somebody else. I am telling you, Brandon and Juan are not what you think they are. I know something about them that I just don't think you know yet."

Marcus looked at his mother with a confused look on his face. He really wanted to know what in the hell she could possibly know about his boys that he did not know. Quickly, it was obvious to Lorna that Marcus was not up on what she was talking about. And she was going to go ahead and tell him.

"I was at this party back whenever," Lorna began. "It doesn't even matter when it was. I was at this party and met some people there that know Brandon and Juan. And I am telling you, they are not your friends like you think they are."

"Mama, what are you talking about?" Marcus asked. "What are you talking about you met somebody at some party?"

"I am bout to tell you, Marcus," Lorna said. "So just calm down. I was at this house party and these people told me that Brandon and Juan used to have some third buddy too. And that third buddy is dead."

The skin on Marcus' forehead immediately began to wrinkle up as he quickly became defensive. "A third buddy?" he asked. "When?"

"I don't know when," Lorna told him. "I guess it was some guy that the two of them was hanging out with back before they knew you or whenever. Well, according to what I heard, some shit supposedly went down, probably a lot like what happened with you and your apartment getting shot up and you getting shot in the arm. Anyway, that friend is dead now…just like you could have been dead if God was not being so good and looking over you and making sure that that bullet that hit you didn't hit a major organ or your face or something."

This was all news to Marcus. It was not that he was surprised that Brandon and Juan had a buddy before him. That in itself was no big deal. However, he started to think that he was sure that if something like that really did go down then Brandon and Juan would tell him. They were too tight for them not to.

Marcus, not wanting to believe what he was hearing, began to shake his head. "Mama, I don't know about that," he said. "You know how people are. Rumors get around and stuff. Just like you used to tell me when I was growing up, you can't believe everything that you hear."

Lorna, with her mouth closed, rubbed her tongue over the top of the front of her teeth. "I know I told you that, Marcus," she said. "I know. And I am not saying that I believe it, but-"

"But what?" Marcus snapped back. "You obviously believe that shit or else you wouldn't even be bringing it up. Look at your face. You are just so convinced that they had something to do with all of this that you are lookin' for any possible connection."

Lorna gave her son a little extra room, considering the fact that he had been shot in the arm. She told herself that him using a curse word like "shit" to her face and while he was sitting in her living room was just because of whatever the hospital had given him. If he were in his right mind completely, he definitely would not be talking to her in such a way.

"Marcus, I know how you must be feeling," Lorna said. "But, okay, let's say that all of that ain't true. Let's say that they didn't have a buddy who was shot and wound up dead and is sitting in some cemetery somewhere, think about this before you head up to Fort Wayne tomorrow. If Brandon and Juan are really your buddies like you say they are – your words, not mine, you know – then why weren't they in that car with you when you drove down south to pick up whatever the hell you picked up? Cause, based on what you say, mind you, this Hakim person is after you and only you for whatever amount is missing. Your boys Brandon and Juan get to go on with their life, even when you move away, or worse, as much as I hate to say that. And as for the little situation, that Miss Tweety or whatever her name is, I told you about messing around with women you know damn well belong to somebody else. You really fucked up if you messed around with somebody like that's chick. This definitely is not the kinda life where you would even wanna do something like that. I don't know what in the world possessed you to even do that."

Marcus sighed, hating now that he had even agreed to tell his mother all of what happened with the deal between he and Hakim. Furthermore, he was coming to the point where talking about it with his mother just did not help him to feel any better about it considering he really did not know what happened to half of the brick of cocaine that Hakim called him alleging was missing. Like he had told Kayla when she was walking him down the hall from getting his arm patched up, and when she was driving him home, he searched all through his car and in the part where the bricks were stashed in case he got pulled over. He simply did not see a speck of anything that was remotely white. Now, however, Marcus could admit that he fucked up when it came to smashing Tweety, Hakim's chick. That was definitely a mistake on his part.

"I don't know, Mama," Marcus said, flatly.

"What do you mean you don't know?" Lorna asked, wanting to really understand what could have possibly been going through her son's head at that moment. "Why would you even go there, especially considering if you know who the fuck you was dealing with? I am not saying that it's right that he wants to blow your head off or anything, but I always...always, always, always...since you were in high school, to be careful with these women and to not go messing around with women you know belong to some other man."

"I know, Mama," Marcus said, in a very tired tone. "I know. But I can't undo it now, so what I'mma do then?"

"We have already talked about what you're gonna do, Marcus," Lorna told him. "I think everything will be just fine if you step away from all of this for a moment and really just distance yourself."

Marcus looked away from his mother. Even though, at this point, he had had some time to think about what it would really mean going up to stay with his cousin Larry in Fort Wayne, he also could not deny how his heart felt. He loved Kayla so much – in a way that many people like to believe that a man cannot love a woman, especially at his age. However, he was also – slowly but surely – starting to feel disgusted with himself in so many ways. Every so often, he would think about how all of this could have turned out so differently. Not only could he have lost his own life when the bullets began spraying into the apartment. Kayla could have lost her life as well. And that was the part that infuriated Marcus. The very thought of one of Hakim's boys' bullets coming into his apartment and killing what was quickly turning out to be the love of his life. He had known her since the two of them were freshman and sophomores in high school. At first, they just flirted for some years – had that long look that people give to somebody they are feeling in the hallways or maybe on the school bus after school. However, as the two of them came closer to graduating, the attraction was getting stronger and stronger. Marcus knew deep down that Kayla was the kind of chick that he could see himself marrying one day. There was no doubt about that.

Lorna must have picked up on the fact that her son was thinking about something that was deeply personal to him. His long silence was something that any mother could notice. Lorna looked over at her son and said, "Marcus, what you thinkin' bout?"

Marcus was reluctant at first to answer. However, at this point, he had nothing to lose by opening up and he knew that.

"Just thinking," he answered. "I am thinking about Kayla."

Lorna stepped back into the room and sat back down onto the couch across from Marcus.

"About Kayla?" Lorna asked. "What about her, Marcus?"

Marcus shrugged then winced, not fully realizing just how painful purposely trying to move his shoulder could be for a while. He reached up and rubbed it before explaining.

"A lot of stuff, Mama," Marcus answered.

"Come on, Marcus," Lorna said. "Tell me. You know I like Kayla. I really do." She smiled.

"I know, I know," Marcus said, almost blushing. He loved the fact that he had a mother who actually liked his girlfriend. In many ways, the fact that his mama liked Kayla made her seem even more like the right girl for him. While he briefly thought about that, the feelings of guilt moved into his mind and his head shook. "I was just thinkin' about how she could have gotten hit with one of them bullets."

Lorna nodded. "Yeah," she said. "That certainly could have happened. And if it would have happened, it sure would not have been the first time. All you can really do is be glad that it didn't happen. That's all you really can do."

"Yeah, I know," Marcus said. "I mean, I just keep thinking about that. Well, I was thinking about that a lot. We got into it when she was dropping me off."

"Got into it?" Lorna asked, clearly sounding concerned. "What did you two get into it about?"

"Well," Marcus said. "She was talking to me and talking about how she is worried that Hakim and his boys might be after her too. Like we told her at the hospital, though, I told her the same thing. Whoever came by her place asking if I was there could have just been a coincidence. You know I be over there and stuff. I know people over there and I know those people know that me and Kayla are together and stuff."

"Yeah," Lorna said. "But you have to understand, I would be scared too. I mean, that is one crazy of a fuckin' coincidence if you ask me. She is a young girl who did not even know that any of whatever you got going on with Hakim and them was going on. Next thing she knows, or so she said to me when we was sitting up in the hospital while the doctors were operating on you and trying to save your life, she was in the bathroom, using the bathroom, when bullets just start flying into the house. No warning, no rhyme, no reason. Why didn't you tell her about all of this when it first happened? Why would you even cheat on her if you really serious about her and stuff?"

Marcus leaned his head back into the top of the couch. "I don't know," he answered. "I guess, with the whole half a brick missing thing, I just thought that it would go away."

"Marcus," Lorna said, now sounding more forceful. "Baby… That just ain't the way that the world work and you have got to know that. Shit like that, especially when it has to do with money, and on top of that you messing around with somebody else's woman, just don't go away real quick. That's why I think you going up to Fort Wayne will be the best thing right now. Out of sight, out of mind, you know what I mean? Move on with your life. Hell, if you give it enough time, and keep your fuckin' nose clean and watch who the fuck you hang out with, you can move on with your life and finally do something different. Next thing you know, that nigga Hakim will probably get caught up in some other shit and either get killed or wind up going to prison or some shit. I hate to say stuff like that, but that is really the way it plays out. The longer you stay out of his sight and out of his way, the more likely shit like that is to happen. And you know these white people love lockin' us up for just about anything."

"Oh I know," Marcus said. "I know that, Mama."

"Right," Lorna said. "But still, why did you and Kayla get into it? Over what?"

"I am going out of town tomorrow, Mama," Marcus simply said. "I guess she think that it's gonna be like the end of us or something. When she was dropping me off, she brought it up and I could tell that she was really bothered by the entire situation."

"Well," Lorna said. "That's understandable."

"I know it is," Marcus said, shaking his head. "I know and I really do feel bad about it. I really do. But she also thinks that I am just leaving her here to deal with whoever might be after her too."

"Well," Lorna commented. "We not even sure that Hakim and his boys are going after her too." She shrugged. "I mean, we really just don't know if that is the okay. I sincerely hope it is not, though, I can tell you that."

"I hope so, too," Marcus said.

"But I like Kayla and I know she is a smart girl," Lorna said. "I know she is going to be smart about this and be watching her back and stuff. But, Marcus, if you don't hear anything else I am saying to you, please hear this. You gotta help to make this right in some way."

"What you mean, Mama?" Marcus asked. "I told you. I ain't take Hakim's stuff like he is saying that I did. I dropped off everything that they gave me down south in his garage just like he said. And as far as what happened with me and his chick, I can't make that right. I can't take that back."

"I know you can't," Lorna said. "I know you can't. But you can keep in contact with her and be honest. You would be surprised how many women will stay with and work with a man if he is just honest about everything. What you should have done, looking back now, was tell her at least that somebody might have been coming after you. She could have very well have been standing in front of that patio door when the bullets started flying. That is just a fact and we can't change that. If you wanna make things work with her, you will figure out a way. Fort Wayne ain't that far away, no way. Hell, maybe she would even move up there with you. I remember you telling me not too long ago that Kayla was having a bit of a hard time looking for a job here. Maybe she would have better luck up there. I mean, I don't know what kind of jobs she out here applying for, but she just might have better luck up there. On top of that, it would be a new place and stuff and I think that kind of change is always good. When I look back at my life, there are so many times that I wished I would have moved away or at least tried to move away." Lorna looked down at the floor as she reflected on the mistakes, choices, and missteps she made during her youth. "You don't wanna look back and wonder, Marcus. You just don't."

"I told her that," Marcus said. "I told her maybe she could come up there and stuff, but you know she don't wanna leave Indianapolis. You know she gotta help take care of her brother and sister."

Just then, Lorna thought back to how Kayla had said that she had to leave the hospital to go home and make sure that her younger brother and sister got into the house okay. Even then, she wondered what that was about.

"She doesn't wanna leave her brother and sister?" Lorna asked. "So what is she now? Like their primary caretaker or something? Where the hell is that mama of theirs?"

Marcus looked at his mother and shook her head. "Basically," he answered. "And I can't lie, that stuff be affecting our time together and stuff all the time. Ever since her mama and daddy broke up, her mama has just been wildin' out, Mama. Like the woman just done gave up on herself and her children and she always gone all night long and stuff, sometimes without even telling Kayla. There were even a couple of nights where Kayla would text me and tell me that she would walk out of her room and into the hallways to go downstairs or to the bathroom or something and she would run into some nigga she had never even seen before. Once, I remember, a dude was just walking down the hall in his boxers when she came out of her room."

Lorna shook her head. It really hurt her heart to have to hear something like that. She knew all too well how dangerous it could be in the world to be a young lady and to have to live with a mother that was like that. She remembered when she knew Kayla's mother, Rolanda, back in the day. And, to say the least, Lorna just did not remember her as being all that classy of a respectable woman.

"That don't make no damn sense," Lorna said, still shaking her head. "No damn sense. That woman. Well, anyway, it is going to have to be up to Kayla to figure out when and if she can break away from that."

"I think she wants to," Marcus said. "But she know that if she leave the city and go somewhere else, because I talked to her about moving to Atlanta earlier today because I had been thinking about it for a second, she said that she knew for sure that her brother and sister's life would basically go to hell."

Lorna shook her head again. She hated hearing when young women, and in some cases men, had to give up their possible life goals and upward mobility to take care of responsibilities that technically are not theirs. "That's unfortunate," she said. "It really is."

Lorna, at a loss for words and feeling rather tired at this point, stood up and began heading back to her bedroom.

"Marcus, I want you do to some real soul searching and thinking and stuff between tonight and tomorrow," Lorna said, stopping just as she was crossing the threshold into the bedroom hallway. "You're going to have to smarten up and prolly do things differently. You almost lost your life today, and everything that happened put the life of your girlfriend at risk too. I really think you need to do some thinking and be a man – figure out how you are going to handle this situation and stay alive. But I promise you this, you are definitely going to need some distance. And, furthermore, I can almost promise you that Brandon and Juan are not who, or what, you think they are. I could be wrong, but I really don't think that I am."

On that note, Marcus watched his mother disappear into the shadowy bedroom hallway. He then heard her bedroom door close. There he sat, feeling a little woozy in his mother's living room. His mind was so busy with thinking that there was just no way that he could go to sleep. As much as he wanted to believe that his mother was wrong about Brandon and Juan, he at least gave some thought to what she had said.

Lorna walked into her bedroom, pushing the door closed behind her. Without even taking her clothes off, she just plopped down into the bed. Normally, she would never get into bed with her clothes on. However, with how she was feeling, she just did not have the strength to go through the motions of taking her clothes off. When her head hit the pillow, Lorna closed her eyes and tried to go to sleep. Just like for Marcus, it was not working for her either. After several minutes, she just accepted that she was going to lie there, even if it meant lying there until she got up the next morning to get on the road.

Once an hour had passed, the house was so quiet that Lorna could practically hear her heart beating – beating like a clock on the wall. Her mind was too active for her to go to sleep, and she thought part of that might have been because she saw her brother Roy today. While she was raising her son, she had always assumed that it would be a good idea to have an older male role model to be in his life and teach him how to be a man. However, she too realized that she had been young and made the wrong choice by letting Marcus grow up to where he got close to Roy. She always knew the kind of life that Roy was involved in, but she never thought that it would come so close to affecting her like this. Soon enough, as the rage built inside of her with her thoughts, Lorna grabbed her cell phone. Not even bothering to look at what time of night it was, she scrolled through her contacts and called Roy.

"Hello?" Roy answered, sounding as if he had just been lying down or maybe even full blown sleeping.

"Roy?" Lorna said. "This Lorna. You got a second."

"Of course, of course," Roy said, sounding concerned. "Wassup? Did you and Marcus make it home okay and stuff? How is he feeling?"

"We're fine," Lorna said. "And yeah, we did. But that ain't why I am calling you, Roy."

"Oh?" Roy said.

"Yeah," Lorna said. "Look Roy, I am not trying to put all of the blame on you for what happened because I know that you were not there and apparently were not a part of all this."

"Yeah," Roy said, clearly sounding as if she was wondering where all of this could be going.

"But," Lorna said. "I do believe that you are the one who got my son caught up in all this lifestyle of dealing drugs and shit. I don't believe, I know."

"Lorna, look," Roy began to say, in a defensive mode.

"I almost lost my child today," Lorna said, holding back a tear. "If you could please, just let me talk some and then you can say whatever the hell you feel like you need to say. Anyway, like I was saying, I know that you are the one who got Marcus all caught up in all of this. And I know you can't go back and undo any of it. And I know that I played a part in it because I knew it was going on and I guess I either just did not want to believe it or just thought that maybe it was for the moment type of things when my child was clearly progressing in this kind of lifestyle. If he wasn't, he would just be one of these niggas standing around on the corner with dime and nickel bags. But not, he, somehow and someway, is getting hooked up with people who got him driving damn near halfway across the country to get cocaine. Like I said, I know you ain't got nothing to do with that part, but you are the one who I know started all of this. So, here is why I am calling you."

"What, Lorna?" Roy asked, in a very flat tone. Lorna could hear the guilt in her brother's voice through the phone.

"When I take Marcus up to Fort Wayne tomorrow," Lorna said. "You betta not contact him or anything, for at least a long time."

"What?" Roy asked, now sounding a little outraged. "That's my nephew."

"I know who he is to you," Lorna snapped back. "I am your sister and he is my child, so I know exactly who he is to you. I didn't call you to go back over the structure of the family tree. I called to tell you that I think whatever kinds of deals you and him have got going, and with whoever, need to come to an end. He could have lost his life today, and it was all based on a lifestyle that he basically learned from his Uncle Roy. And don't even try to come back with no shit like he found it on his own or no other shit like that. You and me both know that that is a damn lie, so just save us both some time. I want Marcus to use everything that happened as a wakeup call and change his life. No more fast money, no more drug dealing. He ain't got to do all that. He is a smart young man who can make his own choices and he can get a job and maybe start his own business or something."

"Lorna, you know I own businesses too," Roy said. "He can come work with my businesses and stuff. He can…"

"No," Lorna said, sternly. "Because I know you, Roy. And I know that no matter how much money them businesses are making for you, you are going to just go right back to dealing drugs and doing that shit like you have always been doing and he would be right there by your side like he has always been. Like I said, and please hear me when I say this, I know that I had a part in this and I really hate that I did. I should have been a better mother, or more forceful, and have said something or something. I don't know why I didn't. But after tomorrow, I really don't want you trying to have a relationship with my nephew anymore."

Lorna could hear Roy sighing through the phone. However, he was not responding.

"Roy?" Lorna asked.

"I am here, Lorna," Roy said. "I am here. And alright. I hear you, I hear you. I get it. It's fucked up, but I hear you."

"Well," Lorna said. "What I find fucked up is how you the one who got my son involved in having this kind of lifestyle, or at least normalized it. But you not the one sitting in there on my couch with a bullet wound in your shoulder. That's the difference, Roy. That's the difference. I don't know how quickly all of this is going to blow over with this Hakim person or whoever, but I am really starting to see that my son's life is in danger."

"Hakim?" Roy asked, now speaking much louder. It almost sounded as if he leaned up from lying down in the bed.

"Yeah," Lorna responded. "That's who Marcus was tellin' me about that he went down south to move some stuff up here for. Some nigga named Hakim."

"Oh shit, Lorna," Roy said. "Fuck."

"What? What?" Lorna asked. Her heart jumped. Suddenly, whatever darkness that was her bedroom engulfed not only her body, but also her soul, her heart, and her thoughts. "What, Roy? You know this Hakim person?"

"Yeah," Roy said. "I know that nigga, I know that nigga. How did Marcus get mixed up with him?"

"Fuck if I know," Lorna said. "Something about him, Brandon, and Juan met him through some other person they know. I don't know, or can't remember all the details right this second. This has been one hell of a day for me, so I'll have to find out more tomorrow or something when I am driving him up to Larry's."

"Lorna," Roy said, in a very serious tone. "I don't know how to tell you this, but…"

"But what, Roy?" Lorna asked. Her voice was now getting louder. "But what? But what?"

"I…" Roy started. "I don't know if Fort Wayne is going to be far enough to get away from a nigga like Hakim. That dude…practically the entire west side knows him and they know him for a reason."

"A reason?" Lorna asked. "What reason is that, Roy? Huh? What reason is that?"

"He don't quit easy, Lorna," Roy said. "That nigga Hakim and everybody he work with goes deep."

Lorna placed her hand on her forehead then glanced toward her bedroom wall – toward the wall that separated her bedroom from her family room. Hearing something like that, especially as a mother, hurt her heart in so many ways. After a few silent moments, she brought herself to ask the very question she really did not want an answer to.

"Roy, do you think that this Hakim person will really keep on until he kills Marcus?"

Her brother Roy was hesitant in answering the question.

***

Kayla's heart pumped again, much like it had been before the two guys walked out of the living room to head to the hospital. Without even thinking, Kayla, Rolanda, and Latrell and Linell went silent. Nobody said a single word. Rather, they all made eye contact – eye contact that was long and unbroken. The look of fear was written across each and every one of their faces.

With her motherly instinct kicking in, Rolanda quickly got Latrell and Linell up and told them to go wait at the top of the stairs. In a matter of moments, the two nine year olds had darted to the top of the steps and were waiting, anxiously, to see what was going to happen next.

Rolanda then rushed over to Kayla, who was still basically frozen in her footsteps with Latrell and Linell's coats in her hands.

Thump! Thump! Thump!

Whoever it was knocked at the door again, telling Rolanda and Kayla that it probably was not the two men. One had come through the back door while the other through the front after barely knocking at all. If they wanted to come back in, they would. Knowing that there was not much time before the two niggas who had basically held them hostage and pistol whipped Rolanda, Kayla knew that they could not just stand there waiting. Just as she was about to say something to her mother, a voice came from the other side of the door.

"Kayla?" the female's voice said. "It's me, girl. It's me."

Kayla's heartbeat dropped immediately as she recognized the voice at the door as being Myesha's. Quickly, she stepped across the room and pulled the door open. "Come in, come in," Kayla said.

Myesha, who was practically shivering from the cold, night wind, stepped inside and they closed the door.

"Girl, I know you said you didn't want me here," Myesha said. "But I had to do something. I am sorry, I am sorry."

"No, it's okay," Kayla said. "It's okay."

Rolanda quickly spoke to Myesha, then told Latrell and Linell to hurry up and come back downstairs so that they could get the hell out of there.

"I saw them leave," Myesha said. "I saw them, but I ain't call the police."

"We gotta hurry up and get outta here," Kayla said. "They gon' be comin' back."

"Coming back?" Myesha asked, clearly alarmed. "What you mean they're coming back?"

"Girl, just what I said," Kayla responded, not meaning to sound snappy. "They prolly gon' be comin' back at any minute, I don't know. We gotta get the hell outta here."

"But why?" Myesha asked. "Why would they be coming back?"

"Cause…" Kayla began explaining. Just then, Latrell and Linell came walking up. Kayla quickly helped the two of them into their coats while Rolanda looked around for hers. When she looked back to Myesha, she finished explaining. "Cause they came asking me what hospital room Marcus was in."

"But you dropped him off at his house, right?" Myesha asked.

"Right," Kayla said, nodding her head. "But I told them that he was still at the hospital, girl. I even told them what room he was in. They left here and headed down there. But before they left, they told us that they would be back if he wasn't in that hospital room. Girl, we gotta get outta here. We gotta get outta here."

"Oh, no," Myesha said. "Where y'all gon go?"

"That's what we still try'na figure out," Rolanda butted in and answered. "I don't know where we gon' go. Let me get my phone so when we get rolling, I can figure out who we can possibly call. I don't know where we gon' go. I gotta get my children outta here, though. I gotta get my children outta here. C'mon y'all, let's get goin'."

Just then, with where Rolanda was standing, Myesha could see the side of her face. Without even thinking, she winced at the sight of the now drying blood.

"What happened to your head, Miss Rolanda?" Myesha asked.

"I got fuckin' knocked in the head with a damn gun," she answered.

Rolanda found her phone setting on the dining room table. She grabbed it and the five of them shuffled out of the front door. Out in the front yard, the snow was starting to build up again. The flurries that had gotten caught in Kayla's eyelashes when she came walking into the house earlier had now become fully grown snowflakes. It did not help that the wind was bitter and sharp and moving quickly. All of them could feel the temperature dropping.

"Myesha, girl," Kayla said, as Latrell and Linell were being shuffled into the car. "I appreciate it all and stuff, but you really should get out of here before them niggas come pullin' back up. Girl, they are crazy. They will do anything and get anyone, as you can see. They forced they way up into the house and held them hostage for a while. I swear, girl. They said they was gon' come back if Marcus wasn't in that hospital room and that there would be bodies on the floor."

Myesha's eyes bugged. "Are you serious?"

"Yes," Kayla said, pushing her best friend toward her own car. "Girl, you betta get outta here. You know Methodist Hospital ain't nothin' but a couple minutes away."

Without even thinking, they both turned to the south and looked at the Indianapolis skyline. In the foreground, where the highway bended and headed into the central area of downtown, sat Methodist Hospital. The complex orange brick building looked so menacing in the winter night that looking at it made Kayla nervous. The hospital emblem, which had always been basically the gateway into downtown, never looked so close as it did at that very moment.

***

Roy wound up talking to his sister Lorna for about twenty more minutes before she eventually got to the point where she was too tired to continue talking. It was agreed that she would be driving Juan up to Fort Wayne in the morning, getting out on the road at least by noon. Roy could not help but to feel somewhat guilty about what his younger sister had said to him. He knew that she was right – right in saying that he was the one who got Marcus involved in this life. Ever since Marcus' father decided to walk out and not be a part of his life, Roy had always seen him as sort of his own son, especially since his own son and daughter were already grown and out in the world on their own. He had stepped in and practically helped to raise the boy when his own daddy would not do the same.

Roy also could not help but to think about how suspicious his sister was of Marcus' boys Juan and Brandon. In fact, after he had told her about Hakim, Lorna had gone on and on during the conversation about how much she just did not care for Brandon and Juan. This was so much so that it got the point where Roy wondered if there was some truth to what his sister Lorna was feeling deep in her soul.

When Lorna called, Roy had been lying in bed in his small one bedroom house on Harding, on the city's west side. From his bedroom, he could hear his neighbors – a group of dudes who had to be no older than Marcus – out on their porch. No doubt they were drinking, and probably smoking. Roy stood up, his tall body towering in his bedroom, and walked over to the window. He peaked out, as he thought about just how deep his nephew Marcus was with Hakim. Roy could not help but to shake his head, wishing that Marcus had never gotten involved with someone like Hakim.

Roy did not know Hakim all that well, and for good reason. When Roy first got into working out in the streets, he was in his late twenties. As a high school dropout with two kids already and what felt like twice as many baby mama headaches, Roy had to make money the only way he knew how. This is when and where his paths began to cross with Hakim's paths and social circles. While the two had never formally met, there was certainly tension between the two of them since their names were both big enough and well-known in the hood. Roy could only wonder why in the world could make his nephew Marcus would want to get caught up with a nigga like Hakim. When he woke up to his phone ringing, his sister Lorna calling, the last thing in the world he ever thought he would hear was the name Hakim. As far as he knew at this point, Hakim had moved up out of the hood and had some nice house way far out, in some suburban subdivision, while his "people" did the low, dirty work down in the city.

Roy walked back over to his bed and grabbed his phone. He decided that it was time to give Brandon and Juan a call. Sure, what Lorna had said to him could very well be true but he wanted to see what the younger cats knew. Furthermore, he wanted to know just what would have gotten

Hakim fired up to the point where he was sending people to shoot up his nephew's apartment out on Shadeland. He called Brandon.

"Wassup?" Brandon answered.

"Wassup little nigga?" Roy said. "What you on?"

"Shit, just chillin'," Brandon responded. "I was just about to hit Marcus up in a minute, but had to handle some business real quick. This chick came through to chill, so you know how that goes."

"Bet," Roy said then let out a little chuckle. "I just got off the phone with his mama."

"Yeah?"

"Yeah," Roy said. "Marcus prolly layin' down sleep right now, but I don't know. But hey, look here, I was seein' what you and your boy Juan was up to and see if the two of you wanna come through and smoke." Roy knew that he needed to sound friendly – as if he were on their level in terms of years– if he wanted to get any relevant information out of them. "That was some fucked up shit that happened to Marcus today and I need to know some things, if you know what I mean."

"Naw, naw," Brandon said. "I feel you on that. We was over here feelin' the same way."

"Oh, yeah?" Roy said. "Is Juan there with you right now? Y'all over at your place chillin'?"

"Yeah," Brandon answered. "When was you wantin' us to come through and shit, Roy?"

"Shit," Roy said, pulling his cell phone away from his face and looking at the time. "What y'all two niggas doin' right now? What y'all up to?"

"Shit," Brandon said, then said something to Juan in the back ground. "We can head over there right now."

"Aight," Roy said, nodding. "I'll be here. Just come up to the door and knock."

"Aight," Brandon said. "We'll be there in like ten, fifteen minutes max."

"Aight."

Roy hung up the phone and slid into some pants and a shirt. He then headed downstairs to his basement. As soon as he got to the bottom of his basement stairs, his Pit Bull, Rocko, ran up to him. Rocko jumped up onto his legs, his tongue hanging out of his mouth as Roy rubbed his hands over the three-year-old Pit Bull's head. Roy then grabbed some weed off of a coffee table and headed back upstairs. As he sat in the living room, waiting to see a car pull up out front, he rolled what can only be described as a really fat blunt. All the while he did this, taking his sweet time as he always did to roll a blunt, he could not help but to start to have a little fear in his heart and soul for his nephew. He knew that Lorna was just trying to do the best thing for her son by getting him to go up to Fort Wayne to stay with his cousin Larry. However, the more Roy thought about it, the more he realized that if Hakim was really after Marcus to where he would be sending people to shoot up his house, Marcus must have done something a little more than simply fuck up with carrying some work up to Indiana from Texas. Something just did not seem right to Roy, and he hoped that Brandon and Juan would be the two to know more about everything. Every so often, while he waited, Roy could not help but to shake his head. He knew that he had always emphasized to Marcus how important it is to watch who you hang with, why you hang with people, and who you do business with. He specifically remembered a time where he and Marcus were at a BBQ restaurant and he had told him that bad shit can happen when you deal with people you really do not know. Roy hated that his nephew had to learn this the hard way. Even more than that, he just was not sure if Hakim was done teaching him his lesson. Of course, he could only hope that he was, but Roy seriously doubted it.

Furthermore while Roy waited, he could not help but to think about what if his sister Lorna was right. What if Brandon and Juan did have something to do with this? Roy thought about it. He then thought about if they did set Marcus up in some way, what their possible gain in doing such a thing could be. Roy also thought about how he really only knew Brandon and Juan through Marcus. However, he had been around enough to know some things about the world and the people who inhabit it. Roy always had thought of himself as the kind of person who could read people very well, especially little niggas from the hood like himself. And he never saw anything in Brandon or Juan's eyes to make him think that they would try to do harm to Marcus.

Within fifteen minutes or so, just as Brandon had said on the phone, he and Juan pulled up in front of Roy's place. They each looked at each other before getting out of the car. Knowing what they knew now, since going and seeing Terrell earlier, everything had changed – their perception, the point of view, everything. In fact, when they had left Terrell so he could go back into the bedroom and handle his business with that thick honey, part of the ride back to the crib was them talking about the idea that maybe Marcus did take the part of Hakim's work if he smashed his chick too, like Terrell had told them. Brandon and Juan, only thinking it to himself and not wanting to say it out loud to the other, both wondered why their boy Marcus would not tell them something like that. As far as they knew, he went down to Texas and came back and there was, seemingly, no issue. Next thing either of them know, they are getting a call about his place done been shot up and he is in the hospital.

Brandon and Juan could also pick up on how much Marcus' mother Lorna did not care for either of them. Yes, she was cordial when she saw them. However, it was obvious that she was grinning and bearing it when she was dealing with them. Brandon had said to Juan that he hoped Miss Lorna did not think either of them had something to do with this. Juan looked back at him and said that he hoped Roy did not think the same. The two walked up the walkway, from the sidewalk to the porch. As soon as the bottoms of their shoes scuffed against the concrete porch steps, they could hear Rocko barking from the basement. Within seconds, the front door was open and they were walking inside.

Roy shook hands with both Brandon and Juan before they all sat down in different parts of the front room. Roy held the perfectly rolled blunt up then the lighter and handed it to Brandon. Part of him wondered if Brandon and Juan were feeling nervous as they sat across from him. He would soon see.

"So, let a nigga know what really happen," Roy came out and said. "What do y'all know about this situation going on with my nephew? Who is he caught up with and how and why?"

Brandon passed the blunt to Juan.

"Roy, man," he said. "It's this nigga name Hakim."

"I know him," Roy said. "Well, I know of him, I should say. So, how did Marcus get hooked up with Hakim?"

"This nigga we know, Roy, named Terrell," Brandon explained. "He a real cool dude… He live over in Haughville, not too far from Sixteenth and Tibbs, though. Me, Juan, and Marcus been knowing this nigga for a little while and he said that he had a way Marcus could make some money if he wanted to. Since he got the cleanest record out of all of us, he would be the one to do it because he wouldn't have the cops breathin' down his fuckin' neck."

Roy was starting to get concerned. He really wondered where this story could be going. He leaned in, listening as the blunt came around to him. He already could see holes in the story. At the back of his mind, Lorna's words bounced around as he looked at Brandon and Juan.

"Yeah," Roy said, nodding his head. "So what was this way that Marcus could make money? If it was such a great way to make some money, why didn't the nigga Terrell do it then?"

"That's the thing," Juan said. "Terrell on them papers, at the moment anyway."

"At the moment?" Roy asked, wanting clarification.

"Yeah," Brandon said. "Some racist ass cops planted some shit on him he said and he working on fighting to have an investigation done. Evidently something must be workin' cause they ain't locked the nigga up yet, so… But I think he might be on house arrest of maybe to where he can't leave the county. I forget."

"Aight then, little niggas," Roy said, not liking how this entire story had been set up. "And how do you all know this? Me and Marcus's family try'na figure out what we gon' do before Hakim and his niggas get to him and put a bullet in his head. I need to know every-fuckin'-thing, feel me? I need to fuckin' know exactly why Hakim is after Marcus. What the fuck went wrong when Marcus drove down to Texas?"

"That's the thing," Brandon said. "Ain't shit go wrong when he drove down to Texas. The shit went wrong when he got back up here… back to Nap. And the fucked up thing is that Marcus ain't even tell us about all that. Me and Juan was wondering why he ain't fuckin' tell us so that maybe we could watch his back or something or see what we heard in the streets before them bullets went flying into his apartment. Man, we rode by that shit earlier, only for a minute, though. That shit wasn't no warning of any kind. Hakim or him and his niggas was try'na kill Marcus."

"Look here little niggas," Roy said, putting the blunt down into an astray. "Y'all niggas shoulda never gotten even fuckin' involved with a nigga like Hakim. I ain't wanna tell my sister when I was on the phone with her earlier, but that nigga Hakim is a vicious ass nigga. I heard, and y'all betta not go repeatin' this shit, but I heard that that nigga they found in the canal over up by Thirtieth Street was some nigga that fucked Hakim over. Like I said, it is only what I heard and I don't know if the shit is true or not, but I wouldn't doubt it. Back in the day, that nigga used to have fuckin' shoot outs with the cops and shit and get away with it, somehow. So, what was the problem when Marcus got back up north?"

"Apparently, some of the shit was missing," Brandon said. "He went down there and got like seven or eight bricks or somethin' and when he dropped the shit off, there was some missing. Like half a brick or some shit was gone. But that ain't all."

"What the fuck you mean that ain't all?" Roy asked. "There's more?"

Brandon and Juan looked at each other – a look that told him whatever the "more" was would really be the cherry on top. Brandon turned back to Roy to finish telling him.

"And, apparently," Brandon said. "Marcus smashed Hakim's chick, Tweety."

Just then, Roy stood up. The shadow of his tall frame reached over Brandon and Juan on the other side of the room.

"What the fuck he do?" Roy asked.

Brandon took a deep breath. "I heard," he said. "I mean, we heard, that some of the cocaine was missing, like I said, and that Marcus smashed his chick and he somehow found out about it. I don't know how Hakim found out about it, but Terrell knew about it, so I'm just sayin'."

"Fuck," Roy said, now pacing back and forth on his side of the room. "Why the fuck would he do some shit like that?"

"She a bad bitch though, I hear," Juan said. "Real bad."

"So what?" Roy asked. "What the fuck that got to do with anything? Marcus need to know who the fuck he dealin' with. Some of the nigga's shit is missing and he fucked his chick. Why the fuck would Marcus do some shit like that and not think for one minute that he was putting his life in danger?"

"I wanna know why he ain't mention none of this shit to us," Brandon said. "I mean, we knew that he did the trip down south, but he didn't tell us anything about there being a problem when he got back. Wait a second…how was there shit missing but that nigga Hakim didn't get him when he was dropping it off? He woulda seen the shit missing then."

"From what that nigga Terrell was saying," Brandon said. "Something happen to where Hakim couldn't be there when Marcus got back into town or some shit. He dropped it off, I think in the garage or on a back porch or somewhere real low key, and I guess that is where he saw the Tweety chick. You know who she is?"

Roy shook his head. "Naw, I don't think so," he answered. "Shit, maybe I do. You know how niggas in this city can be, especially on certain sides of town. We all know each other in some way or some shit. Maybe I do know her by her real name and not that Tweety shit. Y'all, this is some fucked up shit any way you look at it. That Hakim nigga is gon' kill Marcus. I hate to say that, but I'm really startin' to think it."

Roy then glanced over at Brandon and Juan, unsure if whether or not they knew that Marcus would be going up to Fort Wayne in the morning to stay with his cousin. Of course, he could not help but to think about his sister Lorna and her cold, hard words for how much she just did not trust Brandon or Juan. At the same time, Roy just was not getting that feeling from either of them. He could read the looks on their faces and tell that neither of them had any idea what was going on with Marcus until he got shot today.

Roy decided against telling them about the Fort Wayne thing. If they knew, that was fine; if they didn't know, that was fine too. They would probably hear it from Marcus anyway, so there was no need for him to even go there. He was too busy thinking about Marcus.

"Hakim gon' kill that boy," Roy said. "As much as I hate to say it, unless somebody kill Hakim first, he gon' get to Marcus and kill him. Like I said to y'all little niggas, I don't know the nigga all that well, but I can say that I ain't never heard much good about him. Niggas don't mess with him and the ones that do, I don't ever seem to hear much, but again now that I think about it. I don't know, though… My memory is kinda hazy."

Just then, Rocko could be heard barking very loudly downstairs. Already on heightened alert, the idea of Hakim knowing that Roy was related to Marcus crossed through his mind. It was unlikely, but it was certainly possible. Immediately, the three of them got quiet as they all knew that Rocko's barking was signifying somebody walking up onto the property or maybe even the porch. Quickly, Roy stepped across the room and up to the window. Parting the curtain ever so slightly, he could see a red car out front. He then could calm down a little bit, recognizing the car that had pulled up out front as Red's.

Roy stepped over to the front door and pulled it open.

"Nigga, what I tell you about comin' round here without callin' first," Roy said. "Especially this late at night."

Red, who was medium height and slinky looking with a beard that could rival the beard of Rick Ross, stepped into the house. He smiled as he shook hands with Roy and gave him a brotherly hug.

"Nigga, fuck you," he said, now showing that he was a little tipsy. "I fuckin' text your ass and shit and you never responded. Guess you forget that a nigga was gon' be stoppin' through when he got off work, huh?"

"Yeah, man, yeah," Roy said. "Just kind of been a fucked up day for me."

Red looked at Brandon and Juan, then shook their hands. He had met them a time or two in the past, but the meetings had always been in a passing sort of sense. Red pushed the door closed behind him and stepped further into the room. He could not only smell that they had recently been smoking, but he could sense the tension in the room. Things were just a little too serious.

"Damn, what the fuck is up with y'all niggas?" Red asked, looking deeper into Roy's face.

Roy shook his head and looked away as he grabbed the blunt and lighter and handed it to Red. "Man, Marcus," he said.

"Your nephew?" Red asked, sounding as if he was in disbelief. "What happened to the little nigga, Roy? Damn, I ain't never seen you like this."

"He got shot earlier today," Roy told him. "He was in the hospital and shit. He got hit in his shoulder."

"Damn," Red said. "Where he get shot?"

"Nigga, I said in the shoulder," Roy said.

"Nigga, I mean *where* where?" Red said. He then switched to his professional voice from when he used to work in a hotel downtown. "As in the geographic location."

"At his place over on Shadeland," Roy said, sitting back down. "Me and Brandon and Juan right here was up at the hospital earlier and shit. It was sometime early this afternoon and they pulled up and just start shooting at his place and shit. His girlfriend was there and everything."

"Word?" Red said. He leaned against the doorframe to the hallway as he hit the blunt. "That's some fucked up shit. I know his mama, with her sexy ass, is all worked up over this shit."

Roy's eyes cut to Red. "Nigga, what I tell you about talkin' bout my sister like that?" he said.

"Nigga, I can't help that she fine," Red said. "I don't know why you playin' with a nigga and won't get me the hookup and shit like I been tellin' you to do since way back when."

There was a time when Red lived near Lorna and would see her all the time up at the grocery store. Part of the time, she acted like she was halfway interested in Red. Other times, she acted as if she just could not have the time of day for him or anything that he had to say to her.

"Nigga, whatever," Roy said. "We got bigger shit to worry about right now. And yeah, of course she is feelin' some type of way."

"Well, who shot his shit up then?" Red asked.

Just then, Roy took a second to look across the room at Brandon and Juan. They looked at the two older men with eyes that said they really knew so little of the world. Roy looked back to Red.

"From the sounds of it, he got Hakim after him," Roy said.

"Hakim?" Red asked, in an obviously concerned tone. "What Hakim you talkin' bout, nigga? You not talkin' bout the Hakim, is you?"

Roy shook his head. "Yeah, Red," he said. "Hakim, you know, Hakim."

"Damn," Red said. "How the fuck he get hooked up with that crazy nigga?"

Roy glanced around the room, knowing that he needed to play his hand carefully. He had learned a long time ago that no matter how trustworthy somebody seemed, they could always use certain information against you or make your situation even worse by knowing too much.

"Long fuckin' story," Roy said. "But I think Hakim ain't gon' stop until he kill the little nigga. He might already think that he did, but you know I don't know. At this point, it's been years since I ran in them kinda circles and I ain't too keen on trying to jump back into them if you want the truth. I stay over here and worry about me and mines. And now we gotta figure out what we gon' do about this shit."

"Damn, nigga," Red said, his head hanging low. "That's some fucked up shit if you gotta worry about Hakim and his niggas being after you. Shit, if it was me, I might just go ahead and leave town or some shit, I don't know. Fuckin' around with Hakim make you liable to wind up swimming in the White River downtown or some shit."

Roy looked at Red sharply again, letting him know that his rambling was quickly getting to him. Earlier, before he had found out from Brandon that Marcus had been shot, he had arranged for Red to come over when he got off of work and look at some of the new smoke he got in that was down in the basement. Before he finished talking with Brandon and Juan, he needed to go ahead and get Red what he came for so he could get going. Too many people knowing too much would not be a good idea at this point. Roy stood up and walked toward the doorway to the kitchen, with Red following behind so they could get to the basement steps.

"Hold up a sec, y'all," Roy said. "I'll be right back."

On that note, Brandon and Juan watched Red follow Roy into the kitchen and head down to the basement.

"Man, I am just gon' go ahead and say it, fuck it," Juan said, watching how loudly he talked. "You think Marcus took the shit?"

"Naw," Brandon said, shaking his head. He then shrugged. "I mean, I don't even fuckin' know though to keep it one hundred. We ain't even know that he had a problem when he got back from down south, let alone that he smashed the dude's chick, either."

"I was just thinking, though," Juan said. "Terrell said that Hakim found some of the shit missing when he got back into town whenever, after Marcus had dropped it off with Tweety."

"Yeah," Brandon said. "I guess, why?"

"I wonder if she had a little more to do with this than just bein' some pussy for Marcus," Juan said. "You know how females is...how they be acting. They smile in your face, but will turn around and stab you right in your back. Shit, for all we fuckin' know she coulda went back after Marcus left and took some of that shit and just blamed it on him. Even black woman do that blame it on a black guy thing."

"True," Brandon said. "This shit is fuckin' foul, though. What if the Hakim dude really do try to go after Marcus and kill the and shit?"

"What you mean what if?" Juan said. "He done already did that shit. Just think, nigga. If Marcus had been standing somewhere else or something, that bullet could have hit him somewhere else. Hell, he could have been going outside to his car to get something and they pulled up and popped his ass. That fuckin' glass patio door is probably what took some of the pressure of the bullet off from being just a full impact."

"Dude," Brandon said. "We gotta hit up Marcus tomorrow and go see him and shit, tell him that we gon' help his uncle and shit so he ain't gotta worry about some nigga try'na kill him. We can't just not do shit and watch out boy get wiped out like that."

"Nigga, that ain't what I am sayin'," Juan said. "I feel you, though. Let's just see what Roy say when he come back upstairs since he know this Hakim nigga way better than we would. It's fucked up how Marcus smashed his chick when some of his shit just so happened to come up missin'."

"You remember where his mama stay, though?" Brandon asked. "I know she moved since the last time she had that thing where we was over there, but I forget where."

"I remember," Juan said. "Well, I remember how to get to the block where she live. I don't know if I know exactly what house, but I bet if we ride up and down the street and I see the house, I'll know which one it is. I kinda remember what it look like, a little bit."

"Aight then," Brandon said. "We can get up and shit tomorrow and head over there. Marcus, bruh…he betta stay low. You hear what Roy said? About that nigga being found in the canal up by Thirtieth Street and shit?"

"Yeah," Juan said, shaking his head. "Marcus done really fucked up."

Just then, Brandon and Juan could hear the footsteps of Red and Roy coming back up the stairs. The two older cats were talking about the Marcus situation, with Red telling Roy what he knew about Hakim.

"Yeah, I don't fuck with him either," Red said, as he and Roy stepped back into the front room. "I think I might know a couple dudes he hang around with, but even then I ain't sure."

"Yeah, well," Roy said. "I'mma have to see what I can do…go talk to the nigga and shit."

Red walked toward the door. "Man, you just betta be careful with that shit," he said. "Watch how you move when it come to Hakim and shit. I don't wanna see nothin' happen to you."

"Yeah, I'll let you know, nigga," Roy said, shaking hands with Red.

"Thanks for the shit," Red said. He then leaned over and shook Juan's hand then Brandon's. "Let me go on and get home to this woman before she come callin' me talkin' her shit again."

"Yeah, nigga, I'll see you," Roy said.

"Aight," Red said. He then opened the door and stepped out into the snowy winter night. Roy pushed the door closed and locked it. He stepped back over to the couch where he had been sitting.

"Here's what I'mma do... Here's what I'mma do," Roy said, looking at Juan and Brandon. "I want y'all niggas to keep your ears and eyes open and see what you hear out in these streets. Like I was tellin' Red, I'mma have to see who I can get in touch with and go have a talk with Hakim about this shit."

"Oh yeah?" Brandon said. "You think he really gon' come back after Marcus and really try to kill his ass?"

"I can't let my sister loose her only child," Roy said. "I'mma go see that nigga. What I need y'all to do is figure out who his boys are. I know he ain't the one ridin' round and doin' this shit himself. Even with the couple of times I did meet Hakim, he ain't strike me as the kinda nigga who would be doin' his own dirty work. The nigga is elusive if you want the truth. Red said the only time he ever see that nigga is like in the middle of the day, up at the strip club, sittin' off to the side with a drink and shit. So, findin' his ass ain't gon be easy, but I think I can do it."

"Man, if you want," Brandon said. "We can talk to our boy Terrell and shit and see where Hakim be so it can go a lot quicker."

Roy shook his head. "I thought about that," he said. "And I ain't think that that was a good idea. You niggas really need to be watching your back cause I would bet money that Hakim know who the two of you are and that you are connected to Marcus. If your nigga Terrell know enough to be tellin' you about what Hakim is lookin' for Marcus for, then he know enough to go back and tell Hakim. I am tellin' you young niggas, watch your fuckin' back and I suggest you stay low too." Roy knew that he needed to watch his words very carefully while lying and getting Juan and Brandon on track with the right frame of mind when it comes to their thinking. "If Hakim's, or him and his boys, can't find Marcus real soon like they prolly want to," Roy said. "They gon' be lookin' around for whoever might know where he is. Some of his shit is missing and another nigga smashed his chick. I don't think he gon' just let this shit go easy."

Juan and Brandon looked at one another, knowing just how serious all of this was turning out to be. Even though they thought of themselves as tough niggas, the very thought of a couple of dudes, who they did not even know, being out and looking for them just did not sit easy with either of them. When they looked back at Roy, he got a real serious look on his face.

"Marcus prolly don't realize just how deep in this shit he is," Roy said. "And how lucky he is to be alive…for now. Hakim prolly won't stop unless somebody kill him first. He is that kinda nigga. But he bout to see who he fuckin' with. When it come to my family, I don't fuck around."

Chapter 3

When Kayla got into the car with her brother, sister, and mother, she still could not fully understand just how much her world had just been shaken up. Here they were, in the dead of winter, in the middle of the night, having to leave their home. She could only imagine how angry Hakim's boys would feel when they got to Methodist Hospital to find that Marcus was not in the room where they'd been told. Myesha went on home while Kayla got behind the wheel and pulled out of the parking spot. As quickly as she could, without sliding on the slick, snow packed side street, she rolled down Paris before turning off of the street and zigzagging through the neighborhood streets until they were now heading north on Martin Luther King. Kayla looked over at her mother, who held the rag with ice up to the side of her head while she scrolled through the contacts in her cell phone.

"Okay," Kayla said. "So, where was we gon' go, Mama?" Kayla glanced in the rearview mirror and the still-petrified Latrell and Linell. They sat in the back seat, strapped in by their seatbelts, as they looked out of the windows of either side of the car. It was clear to Kayla that the two nine-year-olds were trying to be strong while also being very confused and scared.

"That's what I am try'na figure out now," Rolanda responded. "I am lookin' at who I can call that would let all four of us come and stay with them at the last minute like this. You know I can't call your Aunt Cheryl. She worked at the damn City County Building downtown, so you already know that she is gonna wanna call the police and make stuff even worse."

"Oh, okay," Kayla said. She then thought about Marcus. "Let me call Marcus and tell him about all of this. He need to know what the hell just happened to us."

While driving carefully in the snow, Kayla pulled her own cell phone out of her coat pocket. She quickly looked through her call log until she found Marcus' name. She tapped it with her thumb, then lifted the phone up to the side of her face. She could only hope that Marcus would answer his damn phone, not that his answering would truly make much difference with what was going on.

"Hello?" Marcus answered.

Kayla could clearly hear in Marcus' voice how he must have been falling to sleep or something. His voice sounded low and groggy, and the background at his mother's house was quiet.

"Marcus?" Kayla said. She glanced at her mother.

Instantly, Marcus could hear the fright in Kayla's voice. At that moment, he could no longer be upset with her about how she had basically blamed her for everything.

"Wassup, wassup?" Marcus asked. "Baby?"

"I am here," Kayla responded. "I am here. Marcus, we try'na find somewhere to stay for the night…well, until whenever."

"Why?" Marcus asked, sounding very concerned. "Why the fuck y'all got to find somewhere to stay all of the sudden? You ain't tell me y'all was gon' be doin' that when you dropped me off over here earlier."

"Marcus," Kayla said, glancing in the rearview mirror at Latrell and Linell then over at her mother before putting her full attention back to the road. "When I got back to the house, his boys was there with Mama, Latrell and Linell."

"His boys?" Marcus asked. "What you talkin' bout, Kayla?"

"Hakim's boys," Kayla snapped back, sounding a little defensive. "When I left your place, Myesha called me while I was riding down the street, you know. Anyway, she told me that this black car was sittin' outside of my house when she had left earlier."

"Black car?" Marcus asked, sounding very alarmed.

"Yes, Marcus," Kayla said. "A black car, just like the one you had told me that you had seen rolling up in your parking lot, outside of your apartment building. She told me that she had seen it and didn't think anything of it. When she told me that, I knew something was wrong, so I hurried up and got back home as quick as I could. When I got home and got inside, there they were. Marcus, that shit was so fuckin' scary."

"Okay, Kayla," Marcus said. "Calm down, calm down. So, what happened?"

Just then, Kayla could feel her eyes watering up. What had happened to her and her family was all too scary for her to just calm down because Marcus had told her to.

"When I got in," Kayla said. "They had guns and was basically holding my mama and brother and sister hostage, Marcus. They forced they way up into the house and was holding them hostage."

"What?" Marcus asked, clearly sounding outraged. "Baby, I am so sorry. What the fuck they want with y'all, though?"

"You," Kayla said. "They wanted to know what hospital room you was in, so I told them the number of your room. They told us that if they went down to that hospital and found that you wasn't there, they was gon' come straight back to the house and prolly kill us all. That's why I ain't call the police when I found out that they was there because I knew that they would prolly do the house the same thing that they did to your apartment."

"Oh fuck," Marcus said. "Baby, I am so sorry. I am so, so sorry. But, wait a minute, where y'all headed to right now?"

Kayla glanced over at her mother, who was no talking softly into the phone.

"That's the thing, Marcus," Kayla responded. "We ain't real sure of where we headed right now but we knew that we had to get the hell out of the house before they got back from finding that you wasn't in the hospital room like I had told them you were. You know Methodist ain't nothin' but down the street from where I stay. Any minute now, they could be pullin' back up at the house so we got outta there as quickly as we could."

"Kayla, Kayla," Rolanda said, trying to get her attention. "Turn on Thirty Eighth Street, like you headin' out east or somethin'. I got somewhere we can go now."

Kayla nodded her head, seeing the anguish in her mother's face. "Okay, Mama," she said. "Okay, I will." Kayla put her attention back toward the road and Marcus on the phone. Just as she was about to talk, she felt her mother tap her arm. "Wait a minute, Marcus," Kayla said. She then held the phone down to where Marcus would not be able to hear whatever her mother had to say to her.

Rolanda's lips became very tight a she spoke to her daughter and kept her tone very quiet so Marcus would not hear what she said. "No matter what you do, don't tell that nigga where we headed," Rolanda told her. "For all we know, them crazy motherfuckas could find out where Marcus's mama stay when they get out of the hospital and go after him too while also finding out where we went too. I swear to God, Kayla. You betta not tell that nigga a damn thing about where we goin' before other people know. I don't need that shit happenin' to my kids again, you understand?"

Kayla nodded, fully taking in just how serious her mother was about the safety of her family. "Okay, Mama," Kayla said softly. "I understand. And I won't."

"Aight," Rolanda said. "Head east on Thirty Eighth Street. You remember where my friend Lyesha stay at, don't you?"

Kayla nodded. "Yeah," she answered. "Off Keystone."

Rolanda then nodded as well. "Well we goin' over there," she explained. "But don't pull up out front like we always do. Instead, we gon' go around back and park in the back of her house so don't nobody know we there. When shit like this go down, you never know who might be watchin' your ass. I'mma tell you where to go when we get closer to her neighborhood. Just be careful with this car. And, like I said, don't say a fuckin' word to Marcus about any of this. I don't care what you do, you betta not say a word to him about where we goin', Kayla. We gotta get real ghost cause you don't know how crazy them niggas might be."

Rolanda went back to talking to her friend Lyesha on the phone while Kayla went back to talking to Marcus.

"Hello?" Marcus was saying. "Kayla? You there?"

"I am here, Marcus," Kayla said. "I am here. We just try'na find where we can go tonight. I am so tired."

"Baby, I am so sorry that happened to you," Marcus said. "I really am. Fuck. When my arm get better, I swear I'mma find them niggas. I swear. This shit ain't cool, I swear it ain't. This shit ain't cool."

"Yeah," Kayla said. "It was pretty bad."

"What the two dudes look like?" Marcus asked.

"Well," Kayla said. "One looked like he was kind of Hispanic or Puerto Rican or something, I don't know. He just looked like he was mixed with something is all to me. This was the dude holding my mama at gunpoint and shit. And he was definitely I guess you would say the ring leader of the two because he was doin' the most talkin' and he was the one who was also talkin' the loudest. The other dude, who was holdin' Latrell and Linell over in the corner, you know, when you come in the door and to the right on the side of the couch, was much shorter and darker. Judging by how his clothes fit on him, I would say he was kind of bulky underneath what he was wearing. Do you remember seeing the two dudes that got out of the car earlier before the bullets started to come into your apartment?"

Marcus thought about it for a moment. "Now that I think about it," he said. "Maybe I do. I remember one lookin' like he was a lot taller than the other one. I really didn't get all that good of a look at either one of the nigga's face. All of remember was them stepping out of the car real quick before they pulled out guns and started shooting. Next thing my ass know, I was on the floor and hit in the shoulder."

"This is probably them then," Kayla said. "I mean, I ain't see them when they started shooting either but the half Hispanic lookin' one was definitely taller than the other nigga. Yeah, Marcus. I think this was the same dudes. They really are after you."

Those were words that Marcus just did not want to hear. Basically since he had been released from the hospital, some hours ago at this point, he was really hoping in the back of his mind that Hakim's boys were just trying to scare him. He now knew that this was not the case, however. Suddenly, everything became more serious to him. His heart sank in his chest at the very thought of what his girl Kayla, who he loved so much, had gone through. And it was all because of what was going on between him and Hakim. That was the messed up part to Marcus because Kayla for damn sure did not even have anything to do with any of this. Marcus could feel his anger and rage building in his veins. If his arm were not so messed up right now, on top of how he was feeling with whatever the hospital had given starting to wear off, he would have asked to be dropped back off at his car then go and handle this situation on his own. If nothing else, Marcus hated how helpless he felt about the entire situation. He had never felt this way in his life.

"So, where y'all headed now?" Marcus asked.

Kayla glanced back over at her mother, who was talking quietly into her phone with one hand while she held the rag with ice up to the side of her head with the other. She could not help but to remember the look on her mother's face when she had told her to not tell Marcus where they were going at that very moment.

"We still try'na figure that out," Kayla answered. "We just happy to be out of the house before them two niggas come back. That shit was so scary, Marcus."

"They ain't hurt y'all, did they?" Marcus asked. "Huh, Kayla?"

Kayla took a brief pause before she answered, trying to think of whether or not her mother would want her telling Marcus about it. She knew that if she were not sitting next to her mother, she would tell him everything. However, the last thing she felt like doing right then was making her mother feel any angrier than she already felt. Kayla simply decided that she would wait until she saw Marcus – whenever that was – before she told him that her mother had been pistol whipped in front of her own children.

"When I see you again, Marcus," Kayla said. "I'll tell you everything."

Just then, Kayla noticed that they were starting to get close to Keystone Avenue – a street that runs north and south from one end of Indianapolis to the other. She knew that she needed to go ahead and get off of the phone so she could get as clear of instructions as possibly. Off and on, during the twenty or so minutes since they had pulled out of the parking spot in front of the house, light snow flurries fell from the sky and landed on her windshield. She drove cautiously, not sure how treated the roads were. Kayla noticed that her mother was now off of the phone with her friend Lyesha.

"Marcus," Kayla said. "Let me call you back so I can talk to my mama."

"Aight," Marcus said. "And make sure you hit me back up too, Kayla. Okay? I wanna know that you okay. Make sure you tell me when y'all finally do decide where y'all gon' go so I can at least know that you safe. You know that I am over here worried about your ass, baby. I really want you to know that."

Kayla gulped, knowing that she now would have to watch what she told Marcus. This was going to be harder for her then she would have ever imagined.

"Okay," she said. "I will. Let me hit you back in a minute and see what she got to say."

"Aight."

On that note, the two ended the call. Kayla looked over at her mother. "I swear," she said. "I ain't tell him where we was goin, Mama. I didn't."

"I know you didn't, I know," Rolanda said. "When you get to Lyesha's block, drive passed the front of her house then turn at the next corner, whatever street that is, and we gon ride around to the back. What Marcus have to say?"

Kayla shrugged. "He clearly worried about us, Mama," she said.

Rolanda's head shook. "If the nigga was so worried about anybody but himself, he would have thought to tell you ahead of time, Kayla," she said. "He would have thought to tell you before bullets started flying into his apartment earlier in the day. But, whatever. That's another day for another matter, anyway. Just be careful with how you drivin' and remember what I told you."

"He goin' up to Fort Wayne in the morning still, I guess," Kayla said.

Rolanda looked at her daughter. "Fort Wayne?" she asked, clearly surprised. "What the hell he goin' up there for?"

"He got a cousin up there," Kayla explained. "And Miss Lorna arranged for him to go stay with his cousin until all of this blow over."

"Ain't that some fucked up shit," Rolanda said. Her head shook as she turned away from her daughter and looked out of the window at the small, square houses that made up the neighborhoods around the intersection of 38th and Keystone. "He already done got him somewhere to escape to – somewhere to at least put a little distance between himself and these crazy ass niggas he done got mixed up with while we the ones who gettin' pushed out of our fuckin' house in the middle of the night like some damn refugees or some shit. Ain't that a bitch? I swear."

"Mama," Kayla said. "You know he ain't meant to do this. You know Marcus. You know he ain't meant for us to get caught up in this stuff like that."

"Yeah," Rolanda said, clearly not sounding all that optimistic. "Kayla, you gon' have to understand some things. Sometimes, it ain't about what people meant to do. It's about what happen. And the fact of the matter is that you tellin' me that he gon' be goin' up to Fort Wayne tomorrow, after a night of peace and quiet at his mama house, while we was being held hostage and my ass was gettin' pistol whipped in my own damn home. I don't give a fuck what he meant to do at this point, Kayla. All I care about is what happened. My children ain't gon have no home for at least a minute. I don't even know what we gon' do about school again."

"Mama?" Latrell said from the back seat. "Where are we going?"

Rolanda turned around briefly to talk to her son and daughter, looking them both in their eyes. "We goin' over to your God auntie's house," she answered.

"Are we gon' be living there now?" Linell asked. "Huh, Mama?"

Hearing her nine-year-old sister ask a question like that practically broke Kayla's heart into a thousand little pieces. Kayla could not help but to put some of the blame on herself. Even though she was just as blind as anybody else would be to this situation, she could not help but to feel some guilt. At least, she felt that she should have told her mother that a couple of dudes in a black car had pulled up out front while Latrell and Linell were outside playing in the snow. She could have at least told her mother that these two dudes asked if Marcus was there. Kayla knew that her mother had been around enough to probably have figured out that they would need to get out of the house if two dudes in a black car were pulling up at the house and asking if Marcus was there on the very same day that Marcus' apartment was shot up. How could she not think to tell her mother all of that before heading to the hospital to see Marcus?

"No," Rolanda said, unsure of even the response that she was giving. "We just gon' go over there and spend the night is all. Don't y'all worried."

"Who were those two guys?" Latrell came out and asked. "Why did they come into our house like that, with guns?"

Rolanda hesitated. She was the kind of mother who believed in giving her children only the information that she felt they could handle. However, at the same time, she also made it a point to be the kind of mother who kept it real with her children. She did not want them to grow up inside of a bubble where they were not really aware of things because they were always sheltered from those things. She decided to just lay all the cards out on the table so that maybe her children could at very least use all of this as a learning experience, if nothing else. Rolanda turned back around in her seat, now looking ahead as Kayla drove carefully down 38th Street.

"When you get mixed up in shit you ain't got no business being a part of, stuff like this can happen," Rolanda explained. "That goes for you too, Linell. When you get older and into high school, which I know is kinda far off, you need to be careful with who you dating."

Kayla could not lie to herself. Hearing something like that did hit somewhat of a sore spot inside of her.

"Your sister's boyfriend done got caught up in some stuff and now his shit is affecting us," Rolanda said. "And that's why you need to be careful who you hang with, especially when y'all get older and stuff."

"What did Marcus do?" Latrell asked. "What did he do to where these two dudes would be coming into our house like they did?"

Rolanda took a moment to think before she could come up with an answer to a question like that. "It's kinda hard to explain," she said, not wanting to give them too much information. "But, basically, something went wrong between Marcus and somebody he know and now that somebody ain't happy with his ass. They not happy at all. They try'na find Marcus and they came to our house cause they was thinking that he might be there."

Latrell nodded. "Is that why those two guys came up earlier, asking if Marcus was there?"

Rolanda's eyes opened widely. She looked into the rearview mirror, into the backseat. "What you talkin' bout, Latrell?" she asked, sounding very alarmed.

This was the moment that Kayla was dreading. Her soul felt like it was grinding inside of a machine as Latrell started to explain what had happened earlier.

"When we was outside playing in the snow earlier, those two dudes pulled up in a car and asked if Marcus was there," Latrell said.

"They did what?" Rolanda asked. This was clearly news to her.

"Yeah," Linell said. "They pulled up and asked if he was there. We told them that he wasn't, but we didn't know why they was asking if he would be there."

Rolanda then looked over at Kayla, who she had picked up on as being very quiet during all of this. "Kayla?" Rolanda asked. "Girl, did you know that them niggas came up asking if Marcus was there?"

Kayla really did not want to answer the question, but she knew that she had to. She nodded and took a deep breath. "Yeah," she responded. "I am sorry, Mama. I ain't think that they was gon' come back or anything. When I went up to the hospital, Marcus and his uncle Roy and his mama was sayin' that all of that might just be a coincidence since Marcus is over to the house from time to time and he does know people around there and stuff."

"Oh my fuckin' God," Rolanda said, hyperventilating. Her nostrils flared from how mad she was at her daughter at that moment for not saying anything about this. "Are you serious, Kayla? You knew about this – about them crazy mothafuckas coming by my house earlier and asking if that nigga was there and you ain't tell me?"

"Mama, I know," Kayla said. "I am sorry, I am sorry. I just wasn't thinkin' like that."

"You wasn't thinkin?" Rolanda said. "What the fuck you mean you wasn't thinkin'? You knew that that nigga's apartment had just been shot up and shit and his ass was sittin' in the hospital with a bullet in his shoulder. How could you not think something of it? Them niggas is dumb if they really think that all of something like that would just be a coincidence. I woulda seen straight through that shit and woulda got my kids outta there, at least for the night, so that they would not have to go through no shit like that. Shit, I am the one who got a fuckin' wound on the side of my fuckin' head while you down at the hospital playing Miss Ride or Die for some nigga who bout to head outta town and leave you here to deal with his mess. Girl, keep on drivin' this car before my damn blood pressure goes up or something. I don't fuckin' believe you."

"But Mama," Kayla said. She then glanced over at her mother. It was very clear that whatever words were about to come out of her mouth would definitely mean little to nothing to her mother. Midsentence, Kayla simply stopped talking and looked back to the road ahead of her as she turned onto Keystone Avenue and headed south. Within a couple of blocks, she was turning on a side street, then going around to the alley. She could feel her mother's rage practically jumping across the middle of the car as she slowly turned into the snow-covered alley.

"Please be careful, Kayla," Rolanda said as the car jerked just a little bit. "You see this alley is narrow as fuck and ain't been ran over."

Within minutes, Kayla was pulling the car into a space between Lyesha's garage and the fence that divided her backyard from her neighbor's backyard. Rolanda called her friend. "Yeah, girl," Rolanda said into the phone. "We out back of your house, on the side of the garage like you said."

Chapter 4

Marcus hung up the phone and could not help but to worry about his woman. He loved her so much and the very thought of her having to go through something horrific like that made him feel even more guilty about everything. Even though he knew that the part of the brick that Hakim had said was missing was not because of him, he still felt some responsibility for Kayla being in harm's way. He looked down at his arm, as it was propped up in a sling, and shook his head. Never in his life had he felt these feelings that he felt at that moment.

Marcus had heard his mother on the phone earlier, but she seemed to be off at this point and was now probably asleep. Marcus wanted to go to sleep so badly, but there was just too much on his mind for him to go to sleep. In fact, he had begun to think about how he would be going up to Fort Wayne the next day – going up to some place he knew nothing about and really only had one person there that he knew, and that was his cousin Larry. And he and Larry were not even all that cool now that he thought about it.

After Marcus got up and went to the kitchen to get himself something to drink and some fruit snacks out of the cabinet, he went back and sat down on the couch. He checked his phone to see if Kayla had hit him back up yet because he wanted to know where she and her family were going for the night. He noticed how Kayla still did not know where they were going when he had gotten off of the phone with her. Just as Marcus was thinking about it all, and tearing into the fruit snacks, his phone started vibrating. He looked down and saw that is was a number he knew all too well – a number that he wished he did not know at this point because of everything that had happened.

"Yeah?" Marcus asked, leaning his head back into the couch.

"So now you try'na play ghost, huh nigga?" a man's voice asked. Immediately, Marcus knew that it was Hakim.

"Nigga, what the fuck you talkin' bout?" Marcus asked. "Ain't nobody try'na play ghost. Why the fuck you send them niggas to shoot up my place then fuck with my girl and her family? Nigga, you lucky I don't kill your ass."

A light smirk came through the phone. "Nigga, you don't wanna start talkin' no shit like that," Hakim warned him.

"Hakim, man," Marcus said. "Why the fuck you doin' this shit? Why the fuck you doin' this? I told your ass, nigga, that I ain't take your shit."

"Nigga, I am passed the fuckin' shit at this point," Hakim said. "But don't think I'mma forget about that either. Nigga, you smashed my chick and then gon' try to play it off like ain't nothin' happen. You gon' see what I do to niggas who try to get with my women and shit. You gon' see."

"Man, whatever," Marcus said, starting to feel a little bold. "Fuck you and your chick. Her pussy wasn't even that good no way. I only fucked her because she was throwing the shit at me like she wanted the d…like she been needin' that shit or somethin'. Don't be mad at me cause you can't give her what the fuck she need, evidently."

"Naw this nigga ain't say no shit like that," Hakim said, rhetorically. "Now I'mma really find your ass nigga. I'mma find your ass, nigga."

"Nigga, fuck you," Marcus said, feeling himself get angry. "Why you send your niggas to my chick's house and hold her family like that and shit?"

"Marcus, man," Hakim said. "This shit could all just be so simple. Why don't you come over and talk to a nigga and shit since you wanna talk so much shit through the phone, huh? Why don't you come through so we can talk like men? Funny how you wanna answer this phone and shit after I had a bullet put in that ass and got that ass runnin' scared."

"Nigga," Marcus said. "Why the fuck you go fuckin' with my girl and her family?"

"Oh, you talkin' bout my boys?" Hakim said, clearly sounding sarcastic. "They was just stopping by there and being nice and shit. We just wanted to drop by and see how you was doin'. You girl, Kayla is her name right? She told them that you was still in the hospital and when them niggas went down there, they found that yo ass was gone. She shouldn't have did that shit, nigga. Aw naw… She gon' wish that she had not done no shit like that."

"What the fuck you talkin' bout nigga?" Marcus asked. "With all these threats and shit you makin'."

Hakim chuckled. "Nigga, I ain't the kinda dude who make threats," he said in a very matter of fact way. "My shit ain't no threat. I am just lettin' a nigga know what gon' happen. You may think you can hide or whatever the fuck you doin', but I know people all up and throughout this fuckin' city. You think you gon' hide from me long, you bout to really see shit heat up. You fucked over my money then smashed my chick."

"Don't be mad at me that your dick is little, nigga," Marcus said. "And I told you I ain't take your shit. I told you I ain't take that shit. Why would I do some shit like that, man? Huh? Why?"

"What you got to say don't matter at this point, nigga," Hakim said. "Just know that not only am I lookin' for your ass now, nigga. But I am also lookin' for your chick. I don't do too well when it comes to these lyin' ass hoes. When my boys got down to the hospital, they said they asked a doctor about you and that you had been done checked out. I was like well, ain't that something. Your bitch knew damn well that she was sending my niggas on an empty run to the hospital. She knew that your ass wasn't gon' be there. She knew that shit. Nigga, I can fuckin' guarantee you this. She gon' be sorry that she ever said that shit, I promise you. I heard she thick too."

Marcus felt his heart start to thump in his chest. "Nigga, what the fuck?" he said. "What the fuck you talkin' bout?"

"Nigga, you know what I am talkin' bout?" Hakim said. "My niggas said that your girl is thick in all the right places. And she got an ass that just won't quit. You know how niggas like that shit, especially me. Just give it a little time. I don't mind playin' the little game with y'all little niggas. I know you prolly not thinkin' clearly and shit, but we gon' find you and her real soon. I got some things I can do with her, if you know what I mean. And she'd probably like that shit, too."

"Man," Marcus said. He stood up, now talking into the phone as he paced in front of the coffee table in his mother's living room. "You betta not fuck with my chick. Leave her alone. She ain't got shit to do with this shit, so I don't even know why you playin' like this, nigga."

Hakim chuckled. "All that shit you talkin' now don't matter now, nigga," he said. "Just know that when I find you and her, it ain't gon' be pretty. I fuckin' promise you this, nigga. It ain't gon' be pretty."

"Nigga, fuck you Hakim," Marcus said. "You just some punk ass nigga that mad that I smashed his chick because you obviously can't do it. That's why she was throwin' it at me, that ole tight pussy. Shit was tight like a fuckin' virgin."

Just then, Marcus could hear his mother's bedroom door opening. The creaking of the hinges was so loud at this late hour – at this hour where the entire neighborhood was completely silent. His head quickly jerked and looked toward the bedroom hallway as Hakim was talking.

"Aight then," Hakim said, snickering at the heart that Marcus was showing through the phone. "Just wait till I catch up with you again, nigga. Know that I got my niggas out there lookin' for you, and now that bitch of yours. You can't run forever, and I don't give up to easy either."

"Marcus, who you talkin' to like that?" Lorna asked. She walked out of her bedroom and quickly came down the hallway.

Marcus, now feeling fully angry about Hakim calling him and making suggestive comments about Kayla, did not pay much attention to whatever his mother was saying. He was now getting rather loud as he talked into the phone.

"Nigga, fuck you!" Marcus said to Hakim, almost yelling into the phone. "As soon as my fuckin' arm and shit is betta, I'mma be seein' you before you come seein' me."

"Hang up the phone, Marcus," Lorna told her son as she walked into the living room and approached him. "Hang up the damn phone."

Marcus turned away from his mother as she was grasping for his phone and repeating herself, telling him to hang up.

"You a dead man walking, Marcus," Hakim said, now snickering because he could here Marcus' mother telling him to get off of his phone. "You betta do what your mommy say before you in even more trouble."

If Marcus were a white person, his face would probably be as red as an apple. At this very moment, he no longer felt the pain in his shoulder throbbing. In fact, he could not even pay much mind to his mother.

"Nigga, fuck you Hakim!" Marcus said. "Fuck you. Nigga, you ain't gon do shit. You just mad and shit."

Hakim chuckled. "Aight then, nigga," he said. "We gon' see about that, you hear me? We gon' see about that."

Before Marcus could even respond to what Hakim had just said, Hakim had hung up the phone. When Marcus realized that the phone call had ended, he looked at his phone just as his mother snatched it from his grip.

"Marcus?" Lorna said, clearly having just woken up out of her sleep. "I told you to hang up."

"I don't care," Marcus said. "That nigga call me, makin' threats and stuff."

"Who?" Lorna asked. "Who was that? Tell me, Marcus. What did he say?"

"It was that nigga, Hakim," Marcus answered. His mother could see how angry he was.

"Alright, sit back down, Marcus," Lorna said. "Sit back down on the couch and tell me what he said. Why did you even answer?"

Marcus tried to calm himself down, sitting back down on the couch where he had been just minutes before.

"Kayla called me earlier saying that two of Hakim's boys held her and her family at gunpoint in they house," Marcus explained.

"Are you serious?" Lorna asked, with a surprised look on her face. "When did all of this happen?"

Marcus started to shrug his shoulder but soon winced from the pain at trying to move the shoulder where he had been hit by one of Hakim's bullets. "I don't know, Mama," he said. "She called me saying that it had just happened I guess and that they was leaving the house to go stay somewhere."

"Where they goin' to stay?" Lorna asked.

"I asked her," Marcus said. "But she said that they ain't know yet – something about her mama was trying to figure that out or something."

"What did they go over there and do some shit like that for?" Lorna asked.

Marcus sighed, hating how he really felt like he was at the center of all of it. Furthermore, he hated that his girl and her family had to go through something like that because of him. "She said that they was askin' her what hospital room I was in and stuff. She told them my room number and when they left to head down to the hospital, she got into the car with her mama, brother and sister and they left the house."

Lorna's head shook. She could not help but to imagine how terrifying something like that must be, especially for a mother. Even though she did not necessarily have fond memories of Kayla's mother from back in the day – from back when the two of them were young – she would never in a million years want her to go through something like that. Lorna believed that no mother should have to go through anything like that.

Marcus continued on explaining what all had just happened. "Kayla said she was gonna hit me back when they got settled somewhere or whatever," he said. "That's when Hakim called me, like a few minutes later, if that. He said that when his boys went to the hospital to find me, I wasn't there. He said that he was gon keep lookin' until he find me and stuff, Mama. He just talkin'. He just talkin'. That's all he doin'."

Lorna sat down next to her son, knowing that she needed to talk to him and let him know some things.

"Marcus," Lorna said, feeling the fear that any mother would feel in heart. "I know you're trying to be tough with all of this and stuff, but I think you need to listen to me. If this nigga, Hakim or whatever you said his name is, is going this far…if he is shooting up your place and holding Kayla and her family hostage trying to find out where you are, you really need to stop thinking that he is just fronting about all of this. I hate to tell you this, but I really don't think that is what he is doing at all. That is a lot to be doin' just to scare somebody…a lot to be doing."

They were words Marcus did not want to hear. However, he was a man about it and listened to what his mother was saying as he processed it all. "Yeah," he said. "I know, I know."

Lorna took a brief moment to think about all of this. "Marcus," she said, knowing that she needed to choose her words carefully. "Have you thought about going to the police? This might be too much for you to handle, and it sounds like this Hakim person is gonna be giving you a problem for a long time."

Marcus looked at his mother. He had a hard time even believing the words that had just come out of her mouth. Marcus knew Hakim and the kind of people he dealt with. The very idea of going to the police would definitely be like committing suicide. However, he also knew that the other option, based on what Hakim had said, would also be like committing suicide as well. If he had his way, he would take Kayla and her family and even his own family and all head to Atlanta to get away from all of this. However, he knew that was a proposition that would be easier to think about that it would be to actually go through with.

"Mama, are you serious?" Marcus asked. "You know if we go to the police, it's only gonna make it worse."

"Okay," Lorna said. She stood back up and stepped back out into the middle of the floor. With her hands on her hips, she turned around and looked back at Marcus as she was talking. "Okay, okay, okay," she said. "But I don't see what other option you got. If this nigga is crazy enough to not only send people to your place and shoot it up and shoot you, then go to Kayla's place and do something like that with her family. I don't know that going to Fort Wayne tomorrow is really going to make all of this just go away like that, Marcus."

Marcus knew exactly what his mother was saying. And he thought about it all too as he looked down at the floor, feeling embarrassed, helpless, and even ashamed. "Mama," he said. "Hakim also said that he gon' keep lookin' for me and for Kayla, and…"

Lorna could pick up on the seriousness in her son's tone. "And what, Marcus?" she asked. "And what?"

Marcus looked up and into his mother's eyes. "He kept talking about her body and how good she look and stuff," he answered.

Lorna's head dropped and shook side to side. "Oh my Lord," she said. "Marcus, what have you gotten yourself into? What have you gotten yourself into?"

***

When Brandon and Juan left from chilling with Roy for a minute, the two of them knew just how serious things were getting. They both talked about how they could see it all over Roy's face. He was clearly totally shitty about Hakim and his boys going after his nephew.

"Man, you don't think that nigga gon' go kill Hakim, do you?" Brandon asked as he drove the car down the street.

Juan looked over at his boy. "Shit," he said, shaking his head. "I don't know. I think he prolly gon have to, though."

"Why you say that?" Brandon asked.

"You heard what he said, nigga," Juan said. "And you heard that shit that Terrell told us when we went over to his place earlier. You heard him when he said that Hakim ain't the kinda nigga that is just gon' give up."

Brandon glanced at his boy then back at the road. "Man, this is some fucked up shit," he said. "I think...never mind."

"Naw, what?" Juan asked. "What?"

"I think somebody prolly is gon have to kill that nigga, Hakim, prolly," Brandon said. "It would be betta if somebody got his ass before he get our boy, Marcus."

"Yeah," Juan said. "Your prolly right about that shit, man. You prolly right. Has Marcus text you?"

Brandon shook his head. "Naw," he said. "Has he text you?"

Juan shook his head then as well. "Naw, I ain't heard from him," he said.

Just then, Brandon checked the road to make sure it was clear with no curves coming up before he dug into his pocket and pulled out his phone. "Let's hit this nigga up and see how he doin' and shit," he said. "If he ain't sleep."

Brandon called Marcus, listening to the phone ring. After a couple of rings, Marcus answered.

"Wassup?" he said, clearly not sounding his usual self.

"Wassup, nigga?" Brandon said.

"Shit," Marcus answered. "Just got through talkin' with my mama."

Brandon glanced at the time on his car stereo. "Dang," he said. "Her ass is still up this late at night and shit?"

"Naw," Marcus said. "She woke up when she heard me on the phone. Hakim called."

"Hakim called you, nigga?" Brandon asked, clearly sounding shocked by what he had just heard. "What the fuck that nigga call you and say?"

"That nigga trippin'," Marcus said. "He called me right after I got off the phone with Kayla. Kayla was tellin' me that apparently Hakim's boys – probably the two niggas who shot up my apartment – came to her house and held her family hostage so she would tell them what hospital room I was in. She dropped me off at home like a couple hours ago now I guess."

"Damn," Brandon said. "Is you serious, my nigga?"

Juan tapped his boy Brandon's arm. "What happened?"

"Hold up, Marcus," Brandon said. "Hold up. I am bout to put you on speaker phone so Juan can here, if you cool with that?"

"Yeah, man," Marcus said.

Brandon put his phone on speaker phone then handed it to Juan so that he could hold it while he drove the car.

"Aight, nigga," Brandon said. "Go ahead."

"Wassup, Marcus?" Juan asked. "How you feelin'?"

"Man, this is some straight up bullshit," Marcus said. "Like I was tellin' Brandon, Hakim called me right after I got off the phone with Kayla. Kayla was sayin' that he had them niggas go to her house and hold her family hostage and shit to tell them what hospital room I was in and shit."

"Word?" Juan said, shaking his head. "That is some fucked up shit, man."

"I know," Marcus said. "Kayla was saying that she told them the hospital room number and they left to go down there, but she had already dropped me off at home because the doctors said that because the hospital was having some crowding issues, they needed the beds. Plus, there wasn't much else they could do for my ass no way, or so they said."

"So then what?" Brandon asked as he was turning onto the street where he stayed.

"Kayla said that her and her mama and brother and sister got up out the house as soon as them niggas left cause they said that if they didn't find me in the hospital like she said, that they was gon' come back and shit," Marcus said.

"Damn," Juan said, shaking his head. "That is some fucked up shit, for real nigga."

"Yeah," Marcus said. "Then, like five minutes later, here come that nigga Hakim callin'. He said that his boys didn't find me at the hospital and now they gon be lookin' for both of us…for both me and Kayla."

"What he goin' after your chick for if he got a problem with you?" Brandon asked.

"Man, I ain't wanna tell y'all this cause I swear I ain't do it," Marcus said. "But Hakim think that I took some of his shit when I did that trip up from going down south. I told him I ain't take that shit and whatever he got that day when I dropped it off at his fuckin' garage and his ass wasn't even there was whatever them niggas down in Dallas had gave to me when I left. I told him I ain't take that shit, so I don't even know what the fuck he talkin' bout on that shit."

Brandon and Juan glanced at themselves. Since talking to Terrell, they had already known the story, but both decided that they would play dumb since Marcus was just now telling them for the first time. Brandon nodded as he looked at the phone.

"I mean, damn," Brandon said. "So now he after you cause he said he took some of his shit?"

"Yeah," Marcus said, hesitantly. "But that ain't all he mad at. I smashed his chick while I was there."

Brandon and Juan looked at one another again. They already knew what was about to come out of their boy Marcus' mouth.

"Oh, yeah?" Juan asked.

Marcus took a moment before responding. "Yeah, man," he said. "When I showed up to drop the shit off after gettin' off the road, I called Hakim. This nigga gon' tell me that something came up outta town and that's why he couldn't be there and shit. So, I was like coo. He then gon' tell me that his girl is in the house and that she would come out and let me into the garage so I could put the shit there. I did that... all the shit. That's the fucked up part. I even looked through my car, where they hid the bricks and shit, and I swear to God ain't a spec of white shit nowhere. Not a fuckin' spec. I don't have whatever this nigga was talkin' bout is missin' from what he supposed to have."

Marcus continued on with what he was saying. "So, yeah," he said. "When I was over there, dropping his shit off and stuff, I swear y'all, she was just throwin' it at me. Had an ass that a nigga just couldn't keep his eyes off of. That bitch Tweety is bad."

Brandon and Juan both were deep in their thoughts as Marcus explained, remembering what Terrell had said to the two of them when they went over to his house to find out what was going on and why Marcus' apartment would have been shot up. They both remained silent, deciding to act like all of this was new information to them.

"Man," Brandon said. "Why you ain't tell us that you was deep in some shit like this? Why you ain't tell us?"

"Cause," Marcus said. "I ain't think that that nigga was fuckin' serious about this shit, especially since I didn't fuckin' take anything from him. And I don't know why the fuck that hoe would even tell her nigga that I smashed her. She was throwin' the shit at me like she ain't had no good dick in ages."

Brandon and Juan remained silent. They both knew that this Hakim nigga was not the kind of nigga that either of them would ever want to be up against, let alone actually go through with smashing his chick. They wondered what in the hell would make Marcus do something like that, even if she did look good as hell. Both of their heads shook because now their boy was so deep in some shit that he would not be able to pull himself out of all on his own.

"So, he called you and shit sayin' that he gon keep goin' after you and your chick?" Brandon asked.

"Yeah, nigga," Marcus said. "I told that nigga to go fuck his self and that he just mad that I smashed his chick in a way that he obviously couldn't. Y'all shoulda seen how she was throwing it at me. She obviously wanted the d and shit, and that pussy of hers was tighter than a virgin."

"Damn," Juan said, knowing that it must have felt good. At the same time, though, he would like to think that he would not have done the same thing as Marcus.

"We comin' from your uncle place now," Brandon said.

"Y'all are?" Marcus asked.

"Yeah," Juan said. "We left there not too long ago."

"What he have to say?" Marcus asked. "What was y'all doin' over there?"

"Your uncle called us and shit and asked if we could come through real quick," Brandon said. "He real worried about you and shit. And man, we can't even front no more." Brandon decided to go ahead and tell Marcus about how he and Juan had gone over to Terrell's earlier in the day. "We went over to Terrell's earlier to find out what happened and shit and he told us. Nigga, you in some deep shit. That Hakim nigga ain't playin' with your ass."

Marcus was surprised that his boys had gone and found out, but he was not upset. He simply accepted what Brandon had just said to him and kept the conversation moving. All the while he talked to them on speaker phone, he remembered to not tell them that he was going up to Fort Wayne in the morning. He trusted his boys like they were his brothers, but he knew that his mother did not. Furthermore, the last thing he needed was for Brandon and Juan to tell somebody where he was to only have Hakim and his boys in a whole different city, two hours and some change away, looking for him there too. The very thought of that was a little scary to Marcus. Not only was Fort Wayne probably one third the size of Indianapolis, but it was also the kind of place where Marcus did not know too many people. So, if he did need to run should Hakim and his boys come up there, his options would be limited.

"I know," Marcus said. "I'mma lay low for a minute until I don't know when. I need to find out where the fuck Kayla and her people wound up goin'."

"Yeah," Juan said. "That's some messed up shit if Hakim is sending them niggas after her too."

"Yeah," Marcus said. "So, what my uncle say?"

Brandon and Juan glanced at one another before Juan looked back at the phone and Brandon looked back at the road ahead of him.

"He just said that he gon' have to get out in these streets again and see if he can catch up with that nigga Hakim himself," Brandon explained. "When we went over there, we smoked and chilled for a second and he asked us what we knew about your deal and shit cause he wanted to know what the fuck was goin' on with his nephew. I ain't gon lie to you, my nigga. We told him and shit. We told him."

"Yeah," Marcus said, knowing that his uncle Roy was probably so disappointed in him for doing some deal outside of the family. Then, to have this happen – his apartment getting shot up and a bullet in his shoulder – only made what he had done even worse.

"And he said that he used to cross paths with that Hakim nigga back in the day," Juan added.

"Oh, yeah?" Marcus asked, clearly sounding curious.

"Yeah," Brandon said. "He said he used to fuck up dudes back in the day and shit and that that Hakim nigga ain't nothin' to play with."

"Fuck," Marcus said, knowing that Brandon's words had just confirmed his biggest fear. "Fuck, fuck, fuck."

"Man, where you gon lay low and shit, like you said?" Brandon asked.

"Shit, I am at my mama's house right now," Marcus answered.

"Coo," Brandon said. "If you want, we can come through tomorrow and see you and shit and chill, if you want."

Marcus hesitated. "Naw," he said. "My mama said she gon' take me to my family house, somewhere out south, tomorrow. That don't mean we can't chill, but I just don't know when yet. I'd have to hit y'all up. Tell me this, though… How did my uncle seem when y'all talked to him?"

"Man," Brandon said, shaking his head as he glanced at the phone. "He seem pretty shitty about all of this, I can't even lie. I mean…I think he might go kill the nigga or something."

"Yeah," Marcus said. "It look like that nigga really butt hurt over this shit. Gettin' him before he get me might be the only way."

Juan looked at Brandon. "Yeah," he said. "Nigga, you just betta watch your back and shit in case he find out where you are and come rollin' up on you or some shit within the next couple days."

"Naw, man," Marcus said. "A nigga gon definitely lay low and shit. I am just worried about Kayla. Hakim was talkin' bout how his boys was talkin' bout her body and shit."

"Word?" Brandon said.

"Yeah," Marcus said. "And if he fuck with my chick and shit again, a nigga gon' have to do some shit. I just gotta find out where she stayin' and shit and make sure that she okay. I feel bad as shit about all this. First, she almost coulda got shot and shit when they shot up my place and shit. Now, they go over to her house and hold her family hostage and shit and make them go out into the cold to run from them niggas. This shit is fucked up, for real though."

"Aight then, nigga," Brandon said. "We pullin' up out front of the crib right now, man. We pullin' up. We gon' hit you up tomorrow and shit and find out where you are so we can come chill, if that's cool with you?"

"Yeah," Marcus said, knowing that he was lying. "We can chill and shit."

"Aight then, man, you get some sleep and shit and we'll hit you up tomorrow," Brandon said.

"Yeah, nigga," Juan said. "We'll hit you up tomorrow."

On that note, Juan hung up the phone then handed it back to Brandon.

"Man, can you believe this shit?" Brandon asked.

Juan shook his head before blowing air out of his mouth. "Hell naw," he said. "Marcus really betta lay low."

"And he betta hope that his uncle Roy find that nigga Hakim before Hakim find his ass," Brandon said. "That nigga sound like he crazy…don't sound like he playin' at all."

Just then, Brandon and Juan pushed their car doors open, then headed up into Brandon's place. This was proving to be the strangest, and coldest, winter ever for everybody around Marcus. At the back of each of their minds, they wondered just how far Hakim would go to get their boy Marcus. As they stepped inside and shut the front door, they both began to wonder if Hakim would be coming after them soon too. Naptown was big, but it was not big enough to where Hakim could not find out that they were Marcus' boys if he wanted to know. They both knew that they would be sleeping with one eye open tonight, just in case.

BCPL
Baltimore County
Public Library

Kayla woke up the next morning with her usual headache. However, this time the headache was different. When she woke up, felt as if her head was almost to the point of pounding – getting there, but not quite there yet. It was about seven o'clock when she woke up in her Godmother Lyesha's house. It had been a while since she had slept on a couch – since she was a little kid, really, when she would spend the night with her aunt or uncle. This was, however, back before her mother Rolanda had fallen out with her own siblings. Kayla loved her godmother, but she would have given anything to wake up at her aunt or uncle's house rather than on a couch at Lyesha's.

Kayla rolled over on the couch, her head now facing the middle of the living room. Everything was so quiet. The room was empty and she could see her mother's chest going up and down on the other couch. Kayla was surprised that her mother was not snoring, but she was not going to question what could only be described as a miracle to her. Kayla did love how well decorated her godmother's house was. However, the brand-new carpet, lavender walls, and couches that would only be seen in *Home & Style* kinds of magazines could not make Kayla forget how she ended up her – how she came to a point where she was now sleeping on somebody else's couch.

Kayla picked up her phone to check the time and saw that she had a text message from Marcus. It had come last night, after she had fallen asleep. She had completely forgotten to call him back and let him know something – anything. Kayla opened the message.

Marcus: You mad at a nigga?

Kayla shook her head, not really knowing how she was feeling. She had to focus on her daily survival ritual at this point. When they came into Lyesha's house last night, everyone stayed up for a little bit talking then they all went to sleep: Kayla and her mother on couches in the living room with Latrell and Linell sharing Lyesha's second bedroom upstairs. They did not talk about whether or not Rolanda was going to have Latrell and Linell going to school the day after being held hostage by some crazy fools with guns. That was something else that would soon be on Kayla's mind. However, she needed to play mother first before she even began to think about her situation.

"Mama," Kayla said, as softly as possible. She saw no movement – reaction – from her mother. Instead, she simply continued sleeping in a deep sleep. Kayla needed to wake her up to find out what she wanted to do.

Kayla said "Mama" a few more times. When she saw that she was not getting a response, she slid off of the couch in very angry movements. She really did not feel like getting up, especially if things wound up being to where she was not taking her young and brother to school. Feeling the chill of the front room, from the tiny amount of air sliding underneath the front door, Kayla rubbed her arms as she made her way across the room.

Kayla walked up to her mother and moved her shoulder. "Mama, wake up," she said. "Mama."

"What?" Rolanda said, waking up. "Damn…What, Kayla?"

"You try'na have Latrell and Linell go to school today or what?" Kayla asked quietly. "It's seven o'clock already."

Rolanda opened her eyes a little wider, turning over to where she could look more toward her daughter Kayla. "Fuck," she said. "I ain't even think about that."

"Yeah," Kayla said. "We ain't talk about that last night when we got here."

"Uhh," Rolanda said, trying to wake up enough to think through her morning grogginess. "How many days they done missed this year already?"

"I don't know," Kayla answered, shrugging her shoulders. "Maybe a couple. Not that many."

"You wanna take them?" Rolanda asked. "The side of my head still hurt."

Even in the dimly lit front room of Lyesha's house, Kayla could see the wide make-shift bandage on the side of her mother's head. Instantly, she thought about how her mother had been pistol whipped in front of her children no more than eight hours ago. She could not help but to feel a bit of guilt come over her. Even though all of this was not Kayla's fault, she still felt as if she held some of the blame. She went to sleep thinking about how she wished that she would have told her mother about Hakim's boys riding by and asking Latrell and Linell if Marcus was there, at the house. Kayla knew that she would never forgive herself for not telling her mother that. That piece of information could have really made a difference in how last night played out, and Kayla knew that.

"I'll take them," Kayla said. "I was just askin' if you wanted them to go or what."

"Yeah," Rolanda said. "See if they wanna go. If they too shook up, then they can stay here and not go. It's prolly just better that they go then sit around her all day, but it's really on you. I can't take them no way. The side of my head feels like shit, but I'mma be alright."

"Mama," Kayla said. "You sure you don't wanna go to the hospital? I mean, they can help you in the E.R. or something. What if you get infected or something?"

Last night, Lyesha had asked Rolanda why she just did not go to the hospital about the side of her head. Kayla had agreed with her when the five of them were standing around in the kitchen. However, Rolanda simply kept it real and said that she did not have any kind of health insurance. Latrell and Linell were only insured because of their father's military service from when he was younger. If it was not for that, they probably would not even have had any kind of health insurance.

"Kayla," Rolanda said. "You know I ain't got no insurance. I told y'all that last night."

"So what, Mama?" Kayla said. "You know if you go into through the E.R., they have no choice but to help you. I mean, that white bandage thing on your head even got a little blood on it. What if it get worse or something?"

"You saw Lyesha put alcohol and shit on it last night when we got here, when we was in the kitchen," Rolanda said. "She disinfected it then and we prolly gon' do it today before she gotta leave to go to work. Don't worry about me. Just go on and see if Latrell and Linell are goin' to school and get them ready and shit so that they not in Lyesha's way when she gettin' ready for work."

"Alright," Kayla said.

Kayla walked away and headed upstairs. At the top of the steps, she felt around on the wall for the light switch. She was not used to Lyesha's house because they did not come over to visit her at her house as much as she came over to their house. All that would change now, Kayla thought.

When Kayla found the light and turned it on, finding her way, she headed to the room where Latrell and Linell slept on a queen sized bed. She flipped the light on in the room as she pushed the door close.

"Latrell," Kayla said. "Linell. Wake up y'all. Wake up."

Just then, Latrell and Linell began to wake up. They both looked at Kayla, the crust built up in the crevices of their eyes telling her that they both had been sleeping pretty deeply.

"What?" Latrell said.

"It's time for y'all to go to school," Kayla said. She looked at her younger brother and sister, trying to gage their reaction. If they were too resistant to going, then she would just drop it and let them stay. She wanted to make sure they were not too shook up from last night to go to school.

To Kayla's surprise, Latrell went ahead and began to climb out of bed. He slept in some extra clothing that Lyesha had from when her own children were younger.

"You want me to where what I had on yesterday?" Latrell asked.

"Fuck," Kayla said, the word practically slipping out her mouth. Last night they were so shook up from being held hostage at gunpoint that nobody thought for one minute to get any clothes. They had been so focused on leaving the house that they had basically come to Lyesha's house with just clothes on their back. In so many ways, Kayla could not help but to compare herself and what was happening to her family right now to the refugees she would see on the news every so often over in Europe and the Middle East. Sure, they were not quite the same circumstances; however, Kayla and her family did leave for the sake of their lives.

"That's right," Kayla said. She then turned the light off. "Just get back in the bed, Latrell. Y'all go back to sleep. Don't worry about it. Y'all just gon' have to miss today."

Latrell and Linell, like most kids, did not object. Instead, both of their heads fell back into their pillows and they were quickly falling back to sleep. Kayla pulled the door closed and headed back downstairs. Just as she passed her mother, who she assumed would simply be sleeping, she could hear her mother cough softly.

"Kayla?" Rolanda said, just as Kayla was lying back down onto her couch. "What they say? They don't wanna go?"

"We forgot to get them some clothes when we left last night," Kayla said.

"Damn," Rolanda said, rubbing her forehead. "We sure did, didn't we? Oh well, then, just forget it then."

On that note, Rolanda was already well on her way to being back into deep sleep. Kayla, on the other hand, lay away. At first, she closed her eyes and tried going to sleep. However, after several minutes, and several failed attempts, she knew that she was just probably going to be up. There simply was too much on her mind for her to go to sleep. On top of all that, she was not in her usual environment. Looking around only reminded her more of what all was going on.

Kayla picked her phone up and text messaged Marcus: What time you leavin' today?

She set her phone back onto the floor, knowing that it would probably be a while before she would even get a response from Marcus. Now, she looked up toward the ceiling as the winter sky outside ever so slowly lit up with the morning sun. Shades of orange slowly rose into the sky, showing that snowflakes were falling. Kayla suddenly felt very tranquil, knowing that she would not have to go out into the snow and drive. Instead, her mind took her thoughts and focus to yesterday.

"I don't believe this shit," Kayla said to herself, speaking a lot lower than a whisper.

Marcus was going to be headed to Fort Wayne today. She had known him for years and had basically fallen in love with him a few years ago. Never in her wildest dreams did she think that her dude would suddenly be caught up in something that would lead to him having to move up to Fort Wayne, of all places. Kayla really wished that Marcus would have told her ahead of time that that dude Hakim was accusing him of taking some of his stuff when he came back up from down south not too long ago. She was not sure if the outcome would have been different, but she felt as if she would have at least been able to keep her eyes open for something to possibly happening. This entire situation had basically walked up on Kayla, who was blind. And she just did not like that.

Kayla then started to question herself. Was there a reason that Marcus did not tell her? He had told her other things that she would consider to be "sensitive information" before. She started to wonder why he would feel like he could not tell her that he had gotten into something like this with that Hakim dude. Did he not trust me? Kayla asked herself, in thought. Why would he not tell me? Why would he do that?

Kayla, out of habit, checked her cell phone. Still, there was no response from Marcus. She set her phone back on the floor and went back to looking up at the ceiling and thinking. For whatever reason, she could not help but to replay the entire scene yesterday where she walked into the door and found two niggas with guns holding her family hostage. This, as well, was something that she never in a million years thought that she would see, let alone be a part of. This, as well, proved to be something that would be imprinted in her mind forever...until she was an old woman.

How is our relationship going to be with Marcus up in Fort Wayne? Kayla thought. She had never even been to Fort Wayne, that she remembered anyway. If she had been there, it would have been when she was a little girl or something. She told herself that she could go and see Marcus. However, these thoughts brought around others – thoughts about how long Marcus could possibly be up in Fort Wayne. When she thought of Ms. Lorna's face at the hospital, she knew that she was going to do things in such a way to where her son would be as safe as possible. Safety, in this case, could be him staying up there for quite a while.

Soon enough, Kayla could hear her godmother Lyesha up and getting ready for work. Her footsteps thumped lightly up above as she walked between her bathroom and her bedroom. When Kayla looked through the blinds, out into the snowy outside that was the busy Keystone Avenue, she knew that this day would be just as strange as yesterday had been. It may not be as dangerous, per say, or so she hoped, but it would definitely be just as strange. Marcus would be getting into a car and heading a couple of hours up north while Kayla would have to figure out what she and her family were going to do with themselves. When would they go back to their house over on Paris? How would they know when it was a safe enough time to go back home? They would have to go back home to get some things even if they did decide to stay at Lyesha's house for a little while. How long would Lyesha be okay with her friend and three kids staying with her? There would definitely be a time frame on something like that. Kayla was already ready to go back home.

***

When Marcus woke up on his couch, he noticed how differently he felt compared to yesterday. Any other day, he usually would wake up with morning woody, raging under his bed sheets to get some attention. This morning, however, he woke up feeling a little pain in his shoulder from how he was adjusting. By the time he had adjusted, sleeping on a twin sized bed in one of his mother's spare bedrooms, he was fully awoken. He looked toward the window. His mother's long red curtains were slightly parted – parted enough, however, to let some morning sun into the room. A long ray of light crossed the room, reaching over Marcus' body as he lay on the bed. For him, it felt a little weird waking up at his mother's house. When he moved out, his mother Lorna had lived over on the west side, closer to where Kayla lived. Since his mother moved into this house, which was much nicer and had a bigger yard, Marcus had not spent the night.

Marcus knew how fucked up his situation is. Now, with having slept a good five or six hours during the night, he could look back at the situation and really think about it better. His mind played over and over again that moment when he was standing in front of his patio door, earlier in the day yesterday, and he had seen the car roll up outside. He could not help but to think about how his heart jumped and immediately started to beat faster the very few seconds that he saw Hakim's boys hop out of the car, raise their guns toward his apartment building, and start firing. Marcus could almost feel, on the side of his body, how he fell to the floor when a bullet hit his shoulder.

"I shoulda never did this shit," Marcus said to himself. He was referring to going against his uncle, Roy, and working with somebody that was outside of the family, and smashing Hakim's chick. He knew that doing the latter was just the cherry on top for the entire situation. She looked so good, but was just not worth it now that he looked back. He was the one who was now waking up at his mama's house with his arm wrapped up and in a sling from being shot in the shoulder. It all was just not worth it.

Marcus then thought about how he would be heading up to stay with his cousin Larry in Fort Wayne. It was so ironic how he had been trying to push Kayla to thinking about moving away and it would just so happen that Hakim's boys would pull up at his place and shoot it up. He really did not want things to come to where Kayla had to know what was happening. If Marcus could have his way, Kayla would have never been involved and would have never known anything was wrong. Now he had to think about what was going to happen with his own life. And thinking about such a thing was so hard when the guilt consumed him from knowing that Kayla and her family were held hostage because of him. *Fuck*, Marcus thought.

Soon enough, Marcus could hear that his mother was up and moving around. When he heard her walking, he had assumed that she was coming to his bedroom door. However, she passed right by and headed to the kitchen. Marcus went back to thinking, looking at the window. Earlier yesterday, when he had been texting pictures of his manhood to Kayla, he had just automatically assumed that the two of them would be spending the night together last night since they did not get to do so the night before because of how her mother had left without really saying anything. Oh how things can change in the flash of a moment.

Marcus reached around on the bed, looking for his phone. The last thing that was on his mind last night when he was headed to sleep was how he had told Kayla to hit him back up when they got to wherever they were going. He wanted to see if she ever texted him back. When Marcus found his phone and unlocked it, he saw the text from Kayla. She was asking when he would be leaving. He responded: Don't know yet.

Soon enough, a text message popped up from Kayla, letting Marcus know that she was up too.

Kayla: Ok

Marcus: So, you forget about me or what? Where did y'all end up stayin' at?

A few seconds passed before Kayla responded: One of my mama friend's house.

Marcus: Oh ok.

Marcus set his phone down. He had known Kayla for all of these years. He could hear and feel in her words in her text messages. It was obvious to him that she was still not in a good mood. And he could not blame her for that. He could only blame himself.

Marcus slid out of the bed, readjusting his arm as his feet touched down onto the gray carpet of his mother's spare bedroom. He looked away, knowing that he would normally be stretching right now if he had not just been shot in the shoulder the day before. Instead, he stood up and raised himself up onto the tips of his toes. After hearing his toes and knees crack and pop, he walked around the front of the bed and looked out of the window. The window of this bedroom faced the street. Marcus looked out and up and down the street, looking for a black car to come rolling down the street.

He could only hope to God that Hakim's boys did not find out where his mother lived. If anything were to ever happen to his mother because of him, he would never be able to live with himself.

Once Marcus saw that everything looked good outside, he pulled the curtains together and headed out into the hallway. He found his mother in the kitchen. She sat at the table while a kettle of water boiled on the stove. Marcus immediately recognized that it was his mother's morning ritual of making coffee. When he stepped over the threshold and into the doorway of the kitchen, Lorna looked up at her son.

"Good morning, Marcus," she said, in a very flat tone.

"Morning, Mama," Marcus responded.

Lorna's eyes contact with her son was rather short in comparison to what it would normally be. Instead, she looked back down at some magazine on the table and flipped through the pages. She obviously had not gotten near as much sleep as she normally would. The stress from knowing that she had almost lost her child that day proved to be too much. It had weighed on her mind when she got off of the phone with her brother Roy last night, making it hard for her to go to sleep.

"What time was we headin' up to Fort Wayne?" Marcus asked.

Lorna lightly shrugged. "I don't know," she answered. "I was thinkin' maybe ten o'clock or something like that. Why? You okay with that time or what?"

Marcus thought about it for a second. "I mean," he said. "It's coo with me, I guess."

"What about Kayla, Marcus?" Lorna asked. "You talked to her? Are you trying to see her before you leave?"

Marcus stepped into the kitchen then walked up to the kitchen table. "Yeah," he said. "I mean, I ain't talked to her, but she just texted me back like ten minutes ago."

"Oh, yeah?" Lorna asked. "Where did they wind up goin' last night?"

"She said to her mama's friend's house," Marcus told her. "But that's it. We ain't talk about nothin' else. I can tell that she probably not in a good mood."

"Well," Lorna said. "I wouldn't be either if I was her, if you want the truth. Just tell her what time you leavin' and we can get you to see her and stuff."

"What's gon happen with my car?" Marcus asked. "I can't just leave it sitting over at my place."

"Yeah," Lorna said. "Your car crossed my mind last night when I was layin' in bed and trying to fall asleep. I was thinking we could go get it this morning, but then I thought about how hard it's gonna be for you to drive a car with one arm. Just leave the keys here and I'll get your uncle or somebody to come help me drive it over here and put it into the garage or something. I don't want it setting out on the street or something. One, something could happen to it. Two, somebody could ride by and know that it's your car and know where you are or were. I'd rather not have either one of those two things happen, if you know what I mean."

"Yeah," Marcus said. "Did you talk to Larry?"

"Yeah, I did," Lorna said. "He said to call when we get into Fort Wayne. That way he can go ahead and take his lunch break and come home to let you into his place. He told me there was some road construction or something, but we just gon' worry about that when we run into it. I am tired really, so I might just end up spending the night up there in Fort Wayne rather than driving back today. I don't know, though. We will see."

Marcus nodded. "I see, I see," he said. He then turned around and went back to the room where he had slept. After pushing the door closed, he climbed back into the bed, lying on his back, and grabbed his phone. He messaged Kayla: Can you talk?

Within a few seconds, a response message from Kayla popped up: Not really. My mama sleeping right by me.

"Damn," Marcus said to himself. He then got into a text conversation with Kayla.

Marcus: I am sorry. I shoulda told you about all of this before it all blew up like this.

Kayla: I know, but it's okay. We can't do nothing about it now.

Marcus: I just asked my mama and she said we probably gonna head out and up to Fort Wayne around 10 and shit. What you gon' be doin' today?

Kayla: Well, Latrell and Linell ain't going to school, so I am just laying here on the couch at the moment. I hate sleeping on couches.

Marcus could not help but to feel a little guilty with seeing his girl text something like that to him. He knew that her entire situation was his fault. In fact, last night, it was a struggle for him to go to sleep because he was so busy thinking about what his mother Lorna had said to him. After he got off of the phone with his boys Juan and Brandon, all he could really do was think. He had been so careful to play it off like he was not going anywhere today, right after telling them the full story. He was indeed a little surprised that they had already gone over to Terrell's place then to his Uncle Roy's. Marcus wondered for a moment what they thought of him smashing Hakim's girl, Tweety. He wondered if his boys thought he really did steal Hakim's shit and would want to stay away from him because of it.

Marcus went back to messaging with Kayla after a brief moment of thought.

Marcus: Yeah, I know. I wanna see you before we roll out.

Kayla: Yeah?

Marcus: Hell yeah. I love you. I gotta see you before I go out of town for a little bit.

Kayla: I love you too. And when and where?

Marcus took another moment to think. It would certainly be different for him now, as he would have to adjust to not being with his own car like he had been used to for several years at this point. He hated the idea of depending on someone, especially when that someone was his mama. Since she would be driving today, it would be up to her when and where Marcus could go to see Kayla before they left to go to Fort Wayne.

Marcus: Where your mama friend house at?

Kayla: Off of 38th and Keystone.

"Shit," Marcus said to himself. That intersection was not necessarily far from where his mama stayed. However, it was certainly out of the way when his mother already lived close enough to the highway to where they could drive just a few minutes from her street to an onramp and be on their way up north.

Marcus: I'mma see you today before I leave. I promise.
Kayla: Okay.

Marcus climbed back out of bed and stood up, looking around. He was happy that Kayla had taken him back to his place so that he could get some clothes and whatnot. He quickly picked out something to where today, then went and took a shower. For the first time in his life, he knew the struggle of taking a shower with your arm in a cast and it in a sling. He remembered how the nurses at the hospital had mentioned to him that he would definitely need to be careful to not get water down into the inside of the cast. If he did, he would be itching like crazy and that was something that he just did not want to experience.

When Marcus got out of the shower and went back to the room where he had slept, he struggled to get into his clothes with just using one arm. Soon enough, he did it though and went back out into the living room. When his mother came walking out of her bedroom, fully dressed, and heading toward the kitchen, Marcus stopped her in her tracks.

"Mama?" he said. "Kayla said she stayin' off of Thirty Eighth…Thirty Eighth and Keystone."

Lorna cringed for a second, not liking where this was going. "Okay?" she said, wanting to know more.

"So, I was thinking…" Marcus said. "Do you want to take me over to see her or do you want me to see if there is a way that she can come over here?"

Lorna thought about it for a second, not really knowing which scenario would work out better. "Well," she said. "I was just about to cook a little something before we left, but I got another idea since you said that as a matter of fact."

"What?" Marcus asked, wanting to know.

"Since you said that she stayin' over on Thirty Eighth and Keystone, why don't you see if maybe y'all can meet up at a restaurant over there or something?" Lorna said. "I can get me something to eat and just eat out in the car while the two of y'all eat inside at a table or something for a little bit. We can't be too long, though, because we gotta hurry up and get on the road since your cousin Larry is going to be leaving work when we get up to Fort Wayne so he can come and let you in."

Marcus nodded his head and picked up his phone to text Kayla. "Aight," he said. "That sounds coo. I'll tell her and see what she says."

"Alright," Lorna said. "The sooner, the better, too."

Lorna turned around and went back to her bedroom so she could finish getting ready. Soon enough, she was on the phone with her brother Roy to let him know that they would be leaving out shortly. This was something she never thought she would be doing – taking her son out of town because somebody might be after him. While she did at times shake her head from just thinking about it, she knew that the day she gave birth to her son that she would do anything to protect him. And protecting him was all that she was doing.

***

Roy was just letting his little side piece friend Cherise, who everybody called Cherry, into the house when he heard his phone ring from his bedroom. Immediately, Roy was gentlemanly about his swag. He held Cherry's hand softly as she stepped up and over the threshold and into the living room. Roy loved those mornings that he would wake up to find that he had a text from Cherry, like this morning. She was a thirty-year-old chick from Detroit who had moved down to Indianapolis just a year or so ago. The dark-skinned honey was staying with her cousin, who was a friend of Roy's. Roy had met Cherry when he went to a get together over at the friend's place, on the south side. Instantly, he was head over heels for her body alone. It was like a work of art to him.

Cherry leaned up and kissed Roy quickly, knowing that he would have to step away for a moment to go attend to his business. Quickly, however, Roy could not help himself. He just had to get a handful of her ass before he walked away. In one swift move, Roy had pushed the front door shut, slid his hands down the sides of Cherry's stomach, and to her lower back before dropping them down and grabbing her ass. Cherry giggled, playfully pushing him away.

"Stop, stop," she said, smiling.

"Wait a sec," Roy told her. "Let me get this phone then I'mma be in here in just a sec to take care of that ass."

As Roy started to step away, Cherry reached out and softly grabbed his bulge through his sweatpants. She almost did not want to let go, always loving how full it felt even when he was completely soft. Roy stepped away and headed into his bedroom. He already had figured when Cherry was walking into the door who it could be that was calling him at that time of morning, at close to ten o'clock. The very first thing he thought about this morning when he had woken up was his nephew.

"Hello?" Roy answered.

"Good Morning, Roy," Lorna said, her tone sounding somewhat flat. "How are you?"

Roy hated when Lorna called in the morning. She always talked to him with all of the pleasantries, and sometimes he just did not want to go through all of that to get the conversation going. This morning, he especially did not. As he answered the phone, he looked out into the bedroom hallway and down to the living room. Even from a distance, he could see the ass that Cherry was sitting on. And he was anxious to get into that room and get to popping it. However, Roy also knew how much mental anguish his sister would have to be under. Above everything, he would always respect what a mother is going through.

"I'm aight, Lorna," Roy said. "How you feelin'? Y'all gettin' ready to head up to Fort Wayne yet or what?"

"Yeah," Lorna said. "In a little bit, we'll be leaving out."

Roy could hear in his sister's voice how she was obviously tired or worried or something. He cringed, hating that she had to be feeling this way. "You aight, Lorna? Be real wit me."

"Yea, I'm good, Roy," Lorna asked. "I'm good. Just was callin' you to tell you that yeah, I am about to take Marcus up to Larry's. Was just talkin' to him and he supposed to be textin' Kayla to see if they wanna meet up before we leave the city. I figured that was the least that I could do, with all that she is going through."

"Yeah," Roy said, nodding his head as he glanced at Cherry sitting in the living room. "I know this is not something that she wanted to happen either, but she's young, she'll get over it."

"No," Lorna said. "I'm talkin' about what she is goin' through, personally with her family and stuff and how they done got caught up in this. That nigga Hakim, or whatever his name is, is crazy, Roy. The nigga crazy."

Roy was instantly confused. Since talking to his sister Lorna last night, some things were just not making sense. He also just then thought about how he wanted to tell his sister what he had found out last night when he was talking to Marcus' boys Juan and Brandon. However, he knew to just let Lorna say whatever she was going to say first. That way, he could use that to gage whether or not he would need to tell her all of that, or just keep it to himself and use it with what he was going to do today.

Roy stepped back into his bedroom and pushed the door up, but not completely closed.

"What you talkin' bout, Lorna?" Roy asked. "What you talkin' bout?"

"Look, Roy," Lorna said. "I don't know what kind of stuff Marcus done got himself into. I know what he tellin' me, but I don't know if it's true of if there are parts missing. I'mma just be real, cause you and be both know that niggas like, so there is no point in even faking on that point."

"Aight," Roy said, wanting her to get to the point.

"Roy said the Hakim nigga called him last night," Lorna said.

Instantly, Roy's heart skipped a beat. Soon enough, it was thumping a little harder than usual. However, he remained calm and made sure to listen very closely to what his sister was telling him on the phone.

"Oh, yeah?" Roy said. "And?"

"And," Lorna said, her tone clearly rising a little. "Marcus was saying something or another about this Hakim nigga saying that he wasn't going to stop looking for him and all that kind of stuff. Basically, threatening him and trying to scare him. That tells me that he know now that Marcus ain't in the hospital and that whoever he had shoot up his place didn't kill him when they did it. But that ain't all I'm talking about, though, Roy. When I said I feel for Kayla, her family is basically in fucking hiding right now too."

"What?" Roy asked, sounding surprised. "You fuckin' serious, Lorna?"

"Nigga, yes," Lorna said. "I am serious. Last night, long story short, they were held hostage by a couple of niggas with guns who wanted to know what hospital room Marcus was in. They said something like if they went down to the hospital and found that he wasn't there, which he wasn't because Kayla had just come from out here…from dropping him off…that they were going to come after her too. Marcus was really mad because when Hakim called, he had said something about how his boys who went to her house and basically terrorized her, her mama, and her little brother and sister, had made some comments about her body…suggestive comments, if you know what I mean."

Roy's head shook, knowing exactly what hearing something like that meant. Marcus had smashed Hakim's chick and now Hakim could have very well made it one of his goals now to not only get Marcus, but also get Kayla. Immediately, Roy could see how getting Kayla would be a double win for Hakim – a double win in so many ways.

"That nigga," Roy said. "I know exactly what that nigga try'na do and he just don't realize that he fuckin' with fire. He gon' go after Marcus' girlfriend not only so he can get with her, but also because he knows that if he get a man's woman, be it his wife or girlfriend or anything in between, and the nigga actually cares for the woman, you can and will get a dude to come out of wherever his ass is hiding so you can get him. I talked to Juan and Brandon last night."

Lorna groaned. "Yeah," she said, sounding snappy. "And?"

"And," Roy said in a somewhat authoritative voice. "I know how you feel about them boys, and I swear to God I did not tell them a damn thing about what we got goin' on today, so don't even start up with that shit. You know me better than that, Lorna."

"Okay," Lorna said. "So, what? What are you saying?"

"I'm just saying that I got the full story from them as far as what this Hakim nigga want Marcus for and I don't think any parts of the story are missing," Roy answered. "And like I also said, I know how you feel about them little niggas, but I swear to you, Lorna…I don't think they had anything to do with this. Something is telling me that they did not. Last night, I had them niggas stop by and we had a little chat and shit, over here at the house. I looked them little niggas in the eye. I had a real man to man conversation with the both of them and was really looking not only at how they answered whatever I had to ask them, but also how they reacted to what I was saying and how they looked, or not, at the other one. Like I said, I know, I know, I know…You got a bad feeling about them niggas, and what I just said to you prolly ain't gon' change that, I was just tellin' you that I still got my guard up and shit in case that they do have some shit to do with this. But, Lorna, I really don't think they do."

"Well," Lorna said. "Maybe they don't have anything to do with it, but that's neither here or there if you ask me. Them niggas still might be up to or have been up to some other shit that we don't even know about, Roy."

"I feel you, I feel you," Roy said. "You know where Kayla is hiding out for the moment or what?"

"Yes and no," Lorna answered. "Somewhere over off of Keystone. We're going to go meet up. Well, they're going to go meet up, at a restaurant or something over there. Roy, I'm so worried I don't know what to do with myself. I didn't get hardly any good sleep last night. I swear I didn't. It was like I kept nodding off for short naps, only to wake up and be looking out of my window or something."

Roy balled his fist. He hated hearing that anyone in his family had to basically lose sleep and live in fear because of something they did not even have anything to do with. Hearing all of this only made him more motivated to slither on through his people and connects out in the streets. Indianapolis is a big city, but it is not big enough to stop Roy from finding Hakim if he really wanted to find him. He already knew, though, that he had to be sure to not connect himself to Marcus when doing so. Last night, as he was going to sleep, he had thought about the planning that Hakim must have gone through when he decided that he was going to get Marcus back for the missing product and for smashing his chick – effort that scared Roy at this point. Would it only be a matter of time before Hakim would find out where Lorna stayed and would be sending his boys over to her place to do the same thing that they had done just yesterday to Marcus' apartment? Thinking about this eventually caused him to think about having his sister come stay with him until everything was handled. On the flip side, however, Roy knew that there was no way something like that would work. Plus, he would also have to wonder how long it would take people to figure out that he was Marcus' uncle. Once people figured that out, he knew that whoever knew Hakim would suddenly make themselves known. Hakim was the reason that a lot of niggas were eating good or living in the nicer parts of the city – up out of the hood, so to speak.

"Lorna," Roy said. "I would say to not worry about that, but you already know that it really wouldn't be real. Maybe when you drop Marcus off up north, you could go stay somewhere until you feel safe enough to go back home and stuff. I'mma go see that Hakim nigga today or tomorrow, at the latest. Don't think I'm over here just chillin' and sittin' back while some crazy ass nigga is after my nephew and shit. And I remember what you said, I promise I won't contact Marcus. Maybe this Fort Wayne thing will be a good way for him to get a fresh start and stuff. Meanwhile, while he up there, I'mma handle this Hakim shit."

"Roy," Lorna said. "Don't do no dumb shit that will wind your ass up in prison, locked up."

"Lorna," Roy said. "Fuck all that. I don't think you see how fuckin' serious this shit is. You say I got Marcus involved in this life, right? Okay, okay, maybe I can be a man and own up to that. But…but, but, but…since I got him involved or whatever, I'mma be the one to have his back. I can't just let this nigga Hakim kill mines. Fuck that shit. I'mma try to talk to him like men and shit, you know…real niggas. But if that don't work, I don't know what's gon' happen… And it's probably better that you don't either for that matter. You just worry about keeping you and yours over there safe while I figure this shit out."

Just then, Roy could hear the hinges squeaking on his bedroom door. Quickly, knowing that he was talking about sensitive stuff, Roy jerked back. His eyes feasted on Cherry, causing him to automatically start smiling as his sister Lorna began to talk into his ear.

"What's wrong?" Cherry asked, smiling as she moved closer to Roy, who basically towered over her. She placed her hands on his arms and rubbed his biceps, loving how he was a good combination of muscle and thickness – something that she always liked in dudes that she would mess around with.

Roy shook his head and held the phone away from his body.

"Nothing, nothing," he answered, talking softly. "This my sister."

Just then, Roy could hear that Lorna had stopped talking. He held the phone back up to this ear, knowing that for the last few seconds he had heard her saying something about how they would be on the road to Fort Wayne within a couple of hours or so. Marcus had just stepped into the room and said where they were meeting with Kayla, over off of Keystone.

"Aight then," Roy said. "Be careful today. Make sure all y'all watchin' y'all backs and shit. You don't know how many niggas this crazy nigga may know or have out there. And I don't know, either. Let me get on and shit and I'mma get to callin' round in a little bit to see where this nigga is at."

"Just don't do nothin' crazy Roy and make shit even worse," Lorna pleaded.

"Yeah, yeah," Roy said. "I won't, I won't." Roy thought about how his sister might be singing a different tune if she really knew what Hakim was capable of.

"Alright then," Lorna said. "I'll send you a text or whatever when we get up to Fort Wayne later on."

On that note, the both of them hung up. Roy instantly dropped his phone onto the bed and put 100 percent of his attention toward the thick chocolate honey that was standing just inches away from him. Her body was calling his name.

"Sorry about that," Roy said, apologizing. "That was my sister, Lorna. She going through some shit right now and just needed to holla at me for a sec."

Cherry smiled. "That's aight," she said. Roy leaned down and kissed her as he felt her hand reach out and grab his manhood through his sweatpants.

When their kiss broke, Roy smiled and slapped Cherry's ass. "You ready for some of this dick?" he asked her.

Cherry smiled, then looked down at Roy's growing bulge in his pants. Her silence was enough for him to know that it was time to blow her back out. Without even speaking, Roy grabbed Cherry's waist and moved her around to the side of the bed. As usual, Cherry did not resist. The way she just gave the pussy up to Roy was the very thing that he liked about her the most the least bit. On top of that, she had time to come through and see a nigga when he needed it the most. And she could take dick so much better than a lot of chicks that Roy had messed around with in the last so-many months. The icing on the cake was the fact that she was what he thought of as a chocolate "bunny." Her skin was the perfect dark brown, her eyes were big and bright, and her body looked as if it had been carved just for the eyes of a black man.

"I'm bout to beat this pussy up," Roy said. "I been needin' this shit, I swear."

"Take that pussy," Cherry said as she felt Roy pulling her leggings and shoes off. To help the process, so to speak, Cherry lifted her shirt over her head and tossed it over toward Roy's bedroom dresser. Within seconds, there she stood in front of him – in front of him in nothing but her matching white bra and panties.

"Fuck," Roy said, parading Cherry's neck and chest with kisses. It turned him on more to hear her giggling, as she always did. Quickly, he had gripped Cherry's body tightly. He loved how thin her waist was before her hips noticeably curved out. Her thighs jiggled ever so nicely, as they were fat and smooth. "This body is just what I needed today."

Not wanting to waist anymore time, Roy gently pushed Cherry back until her back was on his bed. Stepping up to the bed, Roy lowered his sweat pants down to his feet and stepped out of them, knowing that he would need to be freed up a little bit so really dig into her like he wanted. When his manhood, now hard and reaching out in front of him, came up to sight, Cherry leaned her head back. "Shit, you got a big dick," she said, the words practically slipping out of her mouth. "This shit is big, nigga."

Roy parted her legs and started to push inside of her. Hearing how she reacted – her deep breaths and moans – only turned him on even more. Roy leaned over and wrapped his forearms around Cherry's back as he continued to slowly push into her, knowing that he did not want to hurt her. At the same time, though, he knew why Cherry came to him: he had the equipment to reach the deep areas that a lot of other dudes just could not. No matter what, he always went balls deep with her and she never complained or seemed like she couldn't take it.

Once Roy felt himself get as far in as he could go, he let out a deep breath. Cherry was grabbing at Roy's chest and neck as she was getting used to him being inside of her. He slowly stroked in and out before finally speeding up. For the next twenty minutes or so, Roy used the stroke of his manhood to take out his frustration. And Cherry loved every minute of it, even having a couple of orgasms that she would not forget anytime soon.

When stroking in the doggy style position, Roy gripped Cherry's waist as hard as he could. Sweat rolled down every part of his body as his eyes filled up on the sight before him: Cherry's big, bouncing chocolate ass. He could feel himself getting to that point.

"I'm bout to bust," Roy said. "I'm bout to drop these kids off in that pussy."

"Okay," Cherry said, her hair looking crazy from her head rubbing against a pillow at the other side of the bed. She had been so lost in the passion that this somewhat older dude was giving. His stroke and how he used his size was definitely something that could compete with a lot of the younger dudes, in their twenties, who were closer to her age. She could even feel Roy digging into her stomach, which was a feeling she wanted to feel every once in a while.

Roy groaned. "Aight then," he said, taking deep breaths. His stroke increased; sweat practically dripped off of his body. He looked up at his bedroom window, with the morning sunshine sliding through the partially opened blinds and causing rays of light to shoot across the bedroom. "Fuck, fuckkk," he said. "I'm cumin', I'm cumin!"

Within seconds, Roy had dropped his kids off as deep inside of Cherry as he could possibly get. Breathing heavily, and feeling relieved – that feeling of relief that a man can only get from getting some good pussy when he gets up first thing in the morning – he slowly collapsed down to the bed. His softening manhood slipped out of Cherry as he looked over at her.

"I told you," Roy said. "I told you I was gon' get in that pussy."

Cherry, who was rubbing her insides, nodded in ecstasy. "Oh shut up, nigga," Cherry said. She then rolled over and put her head onto Roy's chest. She liked how she could practically feel his heart beating when her head was lying against his body. Cherry looked up at Roy's face, noticing how he was not his usual self. Sure, he had really put some work into really giving it to her just then. However, she had spent enough time with him at this point to know when something was up.

"What's wrong, Roy?" Cherry asked.

Roy looked down at Cherry and into her eyes, realizing that he must have been coming across crazy.

"Shit," Roy said. "Nothing. Just chillin'. Whew, I ain't as young as I used to be."

The two of them chuckled.

"Nigga, please," Cherry said, in a very playful way. "I sure can't tell. You sure fuck this pussy betta than a lot of these young niggas out here."

Roy smiled. "Oh, I do?" he asked. "Is that so?"

"Hell yeah," Cherry said. "Put that on everything."

Roy slid his hand up off of the bed, onto Cherry's lower back then around to cup of her butt. "Awe," he said, bashfully. "You got an ass on you. Goddamn." Roy slapped it. "That shit is fat."

Cherry giggled, loving the attention she got from men about her body. She knew that she had the kind of body where she could walk right by just about any nigga in Indianapolis and get his attention. And even if he was walking with his chick, or wife, that did not stop the looks. She always remembered a time she was walking downtown and watched a man practically walk off of the sidewalk and into traffic when she came walking by. However, Cherry considered herself the kind of chick that only gave up the goods to real niggas – to niggas like Roy.

"For real, though," Cherry asked, still thinking about how something seemed up with him. When she had come into the bedroom about thirty minutes earlier, she could tell that Roy was on the phone talking about something serious. And she did not care if he had a girlfriend. In fact, when the two of them had first met, Roy was talking to some chick that was closer to his age. The first time Cherry had ever messed around with Roy was by dropping to her knees and showing him her oral skills…while he was on the phone with his chick that he was talking to at the time. Let's just say that that was the end of whatever relationship Roy had going on with the other chick. From day one, Cherry had hooked Roy – hooked him to the point where she knew that if she came around at the right time, he would break her off with a little piece of change so she could go to the mall or something.

"What is wrong with you today, Roy?" she asked, clearly sounding more persistent. "I could tell that some shit was on your mind when I first came back here. I ain't wanna ask, but I'm just a little worried."

Roy chuckled. At this point in his life, he had learned very well the games of a sexy woman. In so many ways, he hated how he would bring them into his bedroom from time to time because he did not trust them. A lot of this was probably a bad experience from dealing with his child's mother – a woman who had sworn that she was on the pill. Next thing he knew, nine months had passed and he was a daddy.

Roy rubbed Cherry's ass cheeks. "Just got a lot on my mind right now," he said, in answering her question. "Don't worry, though. Everything gon' be okay. I just gotta find somebody to have a little talk in the next couple days."

Roy then looked down at Cherry and wondered. Could she know Hakim? What would the chances be of her knowing him and she was not even from Indianapolis? Furthermore, if she did know that nigga Hakim, that could work against Roy down the road. And he knew that.

"Oh, yeah?" Cherry said. "Who?"

There was no way that Roy was going to answer that now that he knew. "Just this nigga," he said. "My nephew got shot yesterday and I know he would wanna know about it is all."

"No," Cherry said, sounding very concerned. "Is he going to be okay?"

"Yeah," Roy said. He practically beamed as he lay in bed, in the light of the morning sun, with a beautiful young chick. "He alright. He outta the hospital and shit, so that ain't the problem. Just gotta find one of his friends too, now that I think about it. They were real coo and shit and he said he lost the nigga number, and I lost it too."

"Oh, okay," Cherry said. She knew that something was not quite right about Roy's response. However, she was too tired to really give much thought to it. Not only were here insides a little messed up at the moment, she could feel her pussy starting to get a little sore. "You got me sore over here and shit, nigga," Cherry said. "Damn."

Roy chuckled and slapped Cherry's ass. "Awe stop with your complaining," he said, in a very playful way. "You know you like that shit. You like that."

"I ain't say I didn't," Cherry said, smiling.

"I'mma have to get going soon, though," Roy said. "But I'm mad at you."

Cherry lifted her head up and looked dead into Roy's face. "Mad at me?" she said. "What you got to be mad at me about? Huh? What I do?"

"Calm down, calm down," Roy said, rubbing Cherry's ass cheeks. "You always goin' one hundred on a nigga. I'm mad at you because of what you didn't do."

"What I ain't do?" Cherry asked.

"Well," Roy said, glancing down at his lower body. "My dick down there wonderin' why it ain't been in your mouth since you walked in the door. You know how he feel about that."

Cherry smiled then laughed. She playfully slapped Roy's chest. "Nigga, you nasty," she said.

Roy smiled. "You asked me why I'm mad," he said.

Cherry glanced down at Roy's soft manhood, looking bigger soft than some dudes are hard. She grabbed it, feeling how heavy it was for her small hand. Without even talking, and hoping that she could hit the mall up in a little bit, she lowered her head toward Roy's lap. Within seconds, the sound of her slurping his meat filled the room. Roy smiled, glad that the conversation steered away from what was on his mind. He needed to be very careful with who he talked to, and with what he told them.

"Yeah," Roy groaned, knowing that this pleasurable feeling was just what he needed to help with his stress. It would only get worse as the day went on – as he got closer to actually coming to meet with Hakim. "Suck that dick, Cherry. Suck that dick."

CPSIA information can be obtained
at www.ICGtesting.com
Printed in the USA
LVOW10s0349150617

538120LV00018BA/417/P